"IF WE REGAR[D]... THE ANSWER I[S...WE] ARE HEADED STRAIGHT FOR DISASTER ... THAT CANNOT BE PERMITTED TO HAPPEN."

"What young people bring to politics ... is the willingness to face the problems of our day with blunt honesty and forthright courage."

"SOME AMONG US SAY THE NEGRO HAS MADE GREAT PROGRESS—WHICH IS TRUE—AND THAT HE SHOULD BE SATISFIED—WHICH IS NEITHER TRUE NOR REALISTIC."

"Eighty million Americans—and hundreds of millions of other people would die within the first 24 hours of a full-scale nuclear exchange ... This is simply not an acceptable future—an acceptable world for our children."

"WE DID NOT BUILD THE UNITED STATES ON ANTICOMMUNISM."

"Each of our cities is now the seat of nearly all the problems of American life: poverty and race hatred, interrupted education and stunted lives ... To improve the cities means to improve the life of the American people."

"I BELIEVE THAT AS LONG AS THERE IS PLENTY, POVERTY IS EVIL ... AS LONG AS THE INSTRUMENTS OF PEACE ARE AVAILABLE, WAR IS MADNESS."

Other SIGNET Books of Special Interest

☐ **R.F.K. by Dick Schaap.** A compelling narrative by the noted columnist and photographs by Michael O'Keefe, picture editor of **The New York Times** Sunday Magazine, follow the development of Robert Kennedy into one of the most magnetic and controversial political figures of today.
(#T3558—75¢)

☐ **LBJ: The Exercise of Power by Rowland Evans and Robert Novak.** A bold, penetrating analysis of the wheeler-dealer tactics of Lyndon Baines Johnson —how he sought, achieved, and dispensed power. By two Washington political experts and widely syndicated columnists. "Masterly."—**The New York Times** (#Y3441—$1.25)

☐ **THE NEW YORK TIMES ELECTION HANDBOOK, 1968 edited by Harold Faber.** The political experts of **The New York Times** provide an authoritative, informative manual designed to help the public sort out the facts at work in a controversial election. (#Q3419—95¢)

☐ **I PROTEST by David Douglas Duncan.** A powerful condemnation of the war in Vietnam in photographs and text by the world-famous photographer who was assigned by Life Magazine and ABC News to cover the action in Khe Sanh.
(#N3546—$1.00)

THE NEW AMERICAN LIBRARY, INC., P.O. Box 1478, Church Street Station, New York, New York 10008

Please send me the SIGNET BOOKS I have checked above. I am enclosing $_____(check or money order—no currency or C.O.D.'s). Please include the list price plus 10¢ a copy to cover mailing costs. (New York City residents add 5% Sales Tax. Other New York State residents add 2% plus any local sales or use taxes.)

Name_____

Address_____

City_____ State_____ Zip Code_____

Allow 2 to 3 weeks for delivery

A NEW DAY:
Robert F. Kennedy

Edited by Bill Adler

Picture Editor: MICHAEL O'KEEFE

A SIGNET BOOK

Published by
THE NEW AMERICAN LIBRARY

Copyright © 1968 by Bill Adler

All rights reserved

THIRD PRINTING

SIGNET TRADEMARK REG. U.S. PAT. OFF. AND FOREIGN COUNTRIES
REGISTERED TRADEMARK—MARCA REGISTRADA
HECHO EN CHICAGO, U.S.A.

SIGNET BOOKS are published by
The New American Library, Inc.,
1301 Avenue of the Americas, New York, New York 10019

FIRST PRINTING, MAY, 1968

PRINTED IN THE UNITED STATES OF AMERICA

PREFACE

The spring of 1968 will go down in history as a season of momentous, unexpected news developments week after week. Among the most noteworthy of these developments has been Senator Robert F. Kennedy's decision to seek the 1968 Democratic party nomination for President. The world was aware that this young man seemed marked by destiny to contend for the greatest elective political office in the world at some point in his career. But in fact his decision to run in 1968 was a dramatic reversal of position. Accordingly we have proceeded at once to present the American public with this book expounding Senator Kennedy's views. The selections were collected and edited by Bill Adler and his staff. The reader will find the Senator's thoughts on virtually all the great questions of the day. He will also achieve a fuller sense of Kennedy the man, for the concluding section of the book records the Senator's responses in personal situations that have evoked his wit and charm. Here in particular the reader will sense something of that charismatic quality that so distinguished his late brother, former President John F. Kennedy.

> The Publisher
> The New American Library

CONTENTS

ONE:	THE PROMISE OF GREATNESS	9
	A Role for the Future	11
	The New American Revolution	13
	Challenge and Opportunity	16
	The Willingness to Dare	18
	A Commitment to Humanity	21
	Man's Enduring Works	24
	Freedom, Responsibility, and Justice	25
	Under God and Law	28
	World Problems and the Individual	29
	Credos	30
TWO:	TOWARD A BETTER AMERICA	33
	The Urban Dilemma	35
	Racial Problems	40
	The War on Poverty	47
	Education	50
	Youth—The Greatest Resource	55
	The Law	60
	Civic Responsibility	63
	Crime	67
	Violence	73
	Dissent—A Right and a Responsibility	75

The Press	76
Air Pollution	78
Drug Addiction	80
Protecting the Consumer	81
Sports and Athletics	83
Suffrage	86
Medicare—A Realistic View	87
Automobile Safety	88

THREE: **FOREIGN AFFAIRS:**

A REASONED APPROACH	91
America's Role in a World Community	93
A Purpose Beyond Our Shores	97
Peace	100
Nuclear Restraint	101
Communism	103
Foreign Aid	110
Vietnam	114
Latin America	119

FOUR: **THE WIT OF BOBBY KENNEDY** 123

One

THE PROMISE OF GREATNESS

A Role for the Future

... The spirit of willing participation in a common effort is the kind of spirit that has shaped America since its birth. It is the spirit which does not accept the hardships of today as an excuse for the cruelties of tomorrow. It is the spirit which is not bound by the past but is freed for the future—which trusts to the wisdom and effort of the people to build a better nation. That is the kind of spirit which I want to see returned to the United States—and that is why I run for President.

Camden, New Jersey
April 2, 1968

I have traveled across America in the last two weeks; to New York and California, Alabama and Watts, Tennessee and Nebraska and through the West.

I have spoken. I have listened. And I have been enormously heartened and strengthened. Everywhere the American people seek not revenge but reconciliation. They seek, both at home and abroad, solutions of friendship, not force.

They seek an end to the war in Vietnam. Not through withdrawal or escalation, but through a negotiated settlement in which both sides put away the tools of violence and killing, and labor instead at the conference table for an honorable settlement.

This desire for peace is, above all, what they want for the future. They will respect and honor President Johnson, who has sought to take the first step toward peace. They will support his efforts to move toward negotiations. For they know, above all else, that we will not begin the urgent tasks of construction at home, unless we end the bloody works of destruction abroad.

         Camden, New Jersey
         April 2, 1968

Our role in world civilization rests on the fact that our own needs are consistent with the hopes and dignity of others. It rests on the fact that practical and realistic action is consistent with our deepest ideals and convictions. It rests on the fact that the spirit and meaning of this nation will be in jeopardy if we grapple it to ourselves rather than extend it to others. History is a relentless master. It has no present, only the past rushing into the future. To try to hold fast is to be swept aside.

         Columbus Day Dinner
         Waldorf Astoria Hotel
         New York, New York
         October 11, 1966

Our true interest . . . is to help create a world order to replace and improve that shattered when World War I opened the doors to the twentieth century—not an order founded simply upon balance of power or balance of trade, but one based on the conviction that we will be able to shape our own destiny only when we live among others whose own expectations are unscarred by hopelessness, or fear of the strong, or the ambition to master other men.

> Columbus Day Dinner
> Waldorf Astoria Hotel
> New York, New York
> October 11, 1966

The New American Revolution

... Think how our world would look to a visitor from another planet as he crossed the continents. He would find great cities and knowledge able to create enormous abundance from the materials of nature. He would witness exploration into understanding of the entire physical universe, from the particles of the atom to the secrets of life. He would see billions of people separated by only a few hours of flight, communicating with the speed of light, sharing a common dependence on a thin layer of soil and a covering of air. Yet he would also observe that most of mankind was living in misery and hunger, that some of the inhabitants of this tiny, crowded globe were killing others, and that a few patches of land were pointing huge instruments of death and war at others. Since what he was seeing proved our intelligence, he could only wonder at our sanity.

It is this monstrous absurdity—that in the midst of such possibility, men should hate and kill and oppress one another—that must be the target of the modern American revolution.

> Columbus Day Dinner
> Waldorf Astoria Hotel
> New York, New York
> October 11, 1966

The adventure of change may be a tragic adventure for many—a sad uprooting of cherished customs and institutions. Yet change is the one constant of history. It has certainly been the dominating fact in the development of my own country. From the first moment of independence, the United States has been dedicated to innovation as a way of government and a way of life. Not a decade has gone by in our nation's history in which we did not undergo new experiences and seek new challenges. We were born in a revolution against colonialism, and we have been dedicated ever since to a revolution for freedom and progress.

My country has not been alone in pursuing these aims, and, like all countries, the United States has made its share of mistakes. But at its best and its most characteristic, the United States has been, above all, a progressive nation—a nation dedicated to the enlargement of opportunity for those President Andrew Jackson described as the humble members of society—the farmers, mechanics, and laborers.

The United States is a nation dedicated to the emancipation of women, to the education of children, and, above all, to the dignity of the individual. This commitment to "life, liberty and the pursuit of happiness" has inspired the essential motive of our national life—the unceasing search for new frontiers, not only frontiers of geography, but also frontiers of science and technology and social and political invention and human freedom. These are the new frontiers which must be challenged and conquered by our generation—yours and mine. We must meet these problems and still maintain our dedication to democracy and freedom. To do so we must be imaginative and creative—not blindly wedded to the past. How to accomplish this task is the struggle for the people of every country and for the governments of all nations. We in the United States are willing to meet these challenges as I know you are.

We in my country are by disposition and inheritance a people mistrustful of absolute doctrines and ideologies, persuaded that reason and experiment are the means by which free people fulfill their purposes. Yet we live in a century obsessed with ideology—a century that has been filled with leaders persuaded that they knew the secrets of history, that they were the possessors of absolute truth, and that all must do as they say—or perish.

"The Goals of Government"
Nihon University
Tokyo, Japan
February 6, 1962

History knows no inevitability, except as men surrender to their own fears of the future. And a free nation, united behind strong leadership, has no fear. It faces the unknown with anticipation and with faith. And our history testifies to this faith.

We were born in revolution and nurtured by struggle. We are a tough, viable, industrious people who built a great nation in an uncharted wilderness and preserved individual liberty while achieving the greatest prosperity the world has ever seen. We do not look for a battle or search for a fight, but we are prepared to meet our responsibilities.

> American Association for Health,
> Physical Education, and Recreation
> Taft Auditorium
> Cincinnati, Ohio
> April 6, 1962

Challenge and Opportunity

We live today in an era of challenge. This is a time of uncertainty and peril; it is also a time of great opportunity.

The decisions we make as a people, as a government, during the next few years will affect this planet for generations to come. In fact, what the United States does can very well determine the more basic question—whether there will even be generations to come.

All of us are most concerned about the kind of America we want to pass on to our children. Every generation inherits a world it never made; and, as it does so, it automatically becomes the trustee of that world for those who come after. In due course, each generation makes its own accounting to its children.

When our time comes, we want to make sure that

we bequeath to our descendants a better and safer world than the one in which we live today, a world in which people will be free from the terrors of war and oppression, free from the handicaps of ignorance and poverty, free to realize their own talents and fulfill their own destinies.

> "Counterinsurgency"
> *The Pursuit of Justice*

We are a nation which has reached the height of its power and influence at a time when the old order of things is crumbling and the new world is painfully struggling to take shape. It is a moment as fully charged with opportunity as that granted to Columbus or the heroes of the Italian Renaissance. It offers to this nation the chance for great achievement—or perhaps the greatest and most destructive of failures. It is a voyage more hazardous and uncertain than that which we celebrate today. For we seek to cross the dark and storm-scarred seas of human passion and unreason, ignorance and anger. These were as uncharted in Columbus' time as they are today. Yet we have been thrust upon them by our mastery of the continent he discovered and the knowledge his age began. The way is uncertain, and the trip is charged with hazard. Yet perhaps we can say, in the words of Garibaldi to his followers: "I do not promise you ease. I do not promise you comfort. But I do promise you these: hardship, weariness, and suffering. And with them, I promise you victory."

> Columbus Day Dinner
> Waldorf Astoria Hotel
> New York, New York
> October 11, 1966

As we move toward a political resolution of the agony of Vietnam, we can start to redirect our national resources and energies toward the vital problems of our national community. The crisis of our cities, the tension among our races, the complexities of a society so rich and so deprived: all these call urgently for our best efforts. We must reach across the false barriers that divide us from our brothers and countrymen: to seek and find peace abroad, reconciliation at home and the participation in the life of our country, that is the deepest desire of the American people and the truest expression of our national goals. In this spirit I will continue my campaign for the Presidency.

> Overseas Press Club
> New York, New York
> April 1, 1968

The Willingness to Dare

The future does not belong to those who are content with today, apathetic toward common problems and the fellow man alike, timid and fearful in the face of new ideas and bold projects. Rather it will belong to those who can blend passion, reason, and courage in a personal commitment to the ideals and great enterprises of American society. It will belong to those who see that wisdom can only emerge from the clash of contending views, the passionate expression of deep and hostile beliefs. Plato said: "A life without criticism is not worth living."

This is the seminal spirit of American democracy . . . . It is this which is the hope of our nation.

> Berkeley Campus
> University of California
> October 22, 1966

There is no question which does not require . . . new thinking—the same willingness to dare.

We have grown accustomed to fighting for school desegregation in the South; but are we ready to institute the reforms necessary for true desegregation in the North?

We have grown accustomed to building public housing in the ghetto and writing fair-housing laws for our statute books; but will we build housing that Negroes can afford outside the slums and center cities?

We have committed our surplus food to feed the starving abroad, and we have offered to help in curbing population growth; but will we act on the scale necessary to prevent the mass starvation which our present level of effort cannot forestall?

We ourselves must change to master change. We must rethink all our old ideas and beliefs before they capture and destroy us. And, for those answers, America must look to its young people, the children of this time of change. And we look especially to that privileged minority of educated men who are the students of America.

And answers founded on clear and dispassionate thought must be matched to action, rooted to conviction and a passionate desire to reshape the world. It is not enough to understand, or to see clearly. The future will be shaped in the arena of human activity by those willing to commit their minds and bodies to the past. Ralph Waldo Emerson said, "God gives to each of us the choice between truth and repose. Take which you please. You cannot have both."

> Worthington, Minnesota
> September 17, 1966

We have abandoned isolationism and made commitments in every corner of the world; but will we be equally ready to abandon the status quo and associate ourselves with the rising forces of revolution—in Latin America, in Africa, in Asia?

We have made a military commitment in Southeast Asia; but will we now have the imagination and the initiative to develop a program which will not just take lives but save them?

We have the capacity to destroy the world even after being attacked; but even now, will we have the capacity for patience and restraint to save the world after being provoked?

> New York State Society of
> Newspaper Editors
> Utica, New York
> February 7, 1966

To say that the future will be different from the present and past may be hopelessly self-evident. I must observe regretfully, however, that in politics it can be denounced as radicalism or branded as subversion. There are people in every time and every land who want to stop history in its tracks. They fear the future, mistrust the present, and invoke the security of a comfortable past which, in fact, never existed. It hardly seems necessary to point out in the United States, of all places, that change, although it involves risks, is the law of life.

> "Extremism, Left and Right"
> *The Pursuit of Justice*

A Commitment to Humanity

It is not permissible to allow most of mankind to live in poverty—stricken by disease, threatened by hunger, and doomed to an early death after a life of painful labor.... The fact is that the fortunate fraction of mankind now has the technology and the knowledge to improve all these afflictions, and we must seek huge leaps of imagination and effort to shatter the frustrating and resistant barriers between human capacity and human need.

> Columbus Day Dinner
> Waldorf Astoria Hotel
> New York, New York
> October 11, 1966

We have no infallible party, no iron creed, no all-purpose blueprint; we do not propose to chain mankind to a system of false logic. We have instead faith in human intelligence, human will, and human decency; and we know that, in the long run, these are the forces which make history.

Europe and America share great responsibilities to humanity. In meeting these responsibilities, we must both make a full commitment—not just to ourselves but to the other members of the free community less fortunate than ourselves—not just of physical wealth, but, more important, of our minds and spirit.

> "The New Frontier and the
> New Europe"
> Beethoven Hall
> Bonn, Germany
> February 24, 1962

We do not condemn others for their differences in economic and political structures. We understand that newer nations have not had time, even if they so wished, to build institutions relying primarily on private enterprise as we have done. Our privately owned railroads, our airlines, our communications systems, our industries, were not created overnight. These enterprises developed as a result of private initiative at a time when life was far simpler than it is now. We thus had time to permit their slow growth and time to permit the intertwining of many small units into the great systems that the modern age requires, and, under government regulation, time to permit the continuation of private control. In many of the newer nations, government appears to be the only mechanism capable of performing these feats within a reasonable length of time. This we can understand and appreciate. It neither offends us nor can we deem it hostile.

It is the belief that the restriction of individual liberty is essential to economic growth, coupled with efforts to impose that formula on other nations of the world by subversion or force, that we feel is inimical to peace and liberty.

In the unending battle between diversity and dogmatism, between tolerance and tyranny, let no one mistake the American positions. We deeply believe that humanity is on the verge of an age of greatness—and we do not propose to let the possibilities of that greatness be overwhelmed by those who would lock us all into the narrow cavern of a dark and rigid system. We will defend our faith by affirmation, by argument, if necessary, and—Heaven forbid that it should become necessary—by arms. It is our willingness to die for our ideals that makes it possible for these ideals to live.

> "The Goals of Government"
> Nihon University
> Tokyo, Japan
> February 6, 1962

We have seen the unemployed as a problem and provided welfare; but *men* need work. We have seen physical misery as a problem and built housing; but *men* need communities in which to live. And we have seen the residents of these ghettos as afflicted with problems of person and family and prescribed more psychiatrists and social workers and guidance counselors; but *men* need these helpers far less than they need the chance to contribute to themselves, their families, and their community—to stand with pride in themselves and with respect among their fellows.

Without work—and community—and true opportunity to stand as men and citizens, the basic right, the right to be human, cannot be fulfilled.

> New York Pre-White House
> Conference on Civil Rights
> May 11, 1966

Man's Enduring Works

Florence [Italy] is an enemy to pride because it recounts one of the most powerful and constant lessons of history. The wars and conquests, the brilliantly complex politics, and intrigue, the imperative concerns of state, have been covered by the same years which now cloak the colonial empire of Athens and the triumphs of Rome. They did leave an imprint. But it is the idea and paintings, statues, philosophy and knowledge which endure most vividly, shaping and enriching our own lives. They instruct the future that the mastery of transient events, our accomplishments and victories, will ultimately matter less than what we contribute to the liberation of the human spirit.

Nor are the broken manuscripts and works of art simply the creations of our civilization. They are its source and substance. Many forms of life come together in carefully designed societies. Man alone has built civilizations, not just because he is intelligent or skillful, but because he can remember. Through that memory the ideas and revelations of the past enter the structure to which each generation adds. What has been damaged or destroyed in Florence is part of the fragile fabric of collective memory which binds our conflicting aims and actions into civilization.

Even this does not completely tell us why, in a world filled with destruction and tragedy, the flood of Florence should compel the concern of men and women in so many countries. In an age which has seen entire cities shattered in a moment and millions murdered by cold insanity, why does the sight of a stained painting or a broken door panel call forth sorrow and the pain of loss? It is not simply that the art and records are beautiful and priceless and irreplaceable. It is, rather, that they help redeem us from the terrible judgement of history on the wisdom and love of men. Man has built bombs, but he has also painted the crucifixion. He has expended rage in slaughter, but he has also labored to carve panels for a church or illuminate a manuscript. He must admit to cruelty and injustice, but he can point to Florence and say, "This also is our work."

> Clarion Concert for Italian Flood Relief
> Carnegie Hall
> New York, New York
> January 6, 1967

Freedom, Responsibility, and Justice

If freedom is to be meaningful, independence must be accomplished by the desire to forge a nation patterned upon the people's desires. Otherwise, freedom can be meaningless in its motives and futile in its operation. And the land will be left prey to forces both within and without which would destroy the very freedom which the people seek.

> University of Indonesia
> Djakarta, Indonesia
> February 14, 1962

... Whenever men take the law into their own hands, the loser is the law—and when the law loses, freedom languishes.

This by now should be clear to all Americans. It should be clear that the smallest county courthouse in Alabama and the august chambers of the Supreme Court of the United States must be dedicated to the same purpose—to maintain the individual's fundamental rights. It should be clear that, if one man's rights are denied, the rights of all are in danger—that if one man is denied equal protection of the law, we cannot be sure that we will enjoy freedom of speech or any other of our fundamental rights. That was what was at stake when the Freedom Riders ventured into Alabama.

Laws can embody standards; governments can enforce laws—but the final task is not a task for government. It is a task for each and every one of us. Every time we turn our heads the other way when we see the law flouted—when we tolerate what we know to be wrong—when we close our eyes and ears to the corrupt because we are too busy, or too frightened—when we fail to speak up and speak out—we strike a blow against freedom and decency and justice.

... My faith is that Americans are not an inert people.

My conviction is that we are rising as a people to

confront the hard challenges of our age—and that we know that the hardest challenges are often those within ourselves.

My confidence is that, as we strive constantly to meet the exacting standards of our national tradition, we will liberate a moral energy within our nation which will transform America's role and America's influence throughout the world—and that upon this release of energy depends the world's hope for peace, freedom, and justice everywhere.

> Joint Defense Appeal of the
> American Jewish Committee and
> the Anti-Defamation League of
> the B'nai B'rith
> Chicago, Illinois
> June 21, 1961

Our system *can* correct injustice, because freedom of action in America carries with it civic responsibility. And the truth is that we must correct injustice, not because of a bad press around the world, but because it *is* injustice.

The damage done to the United States in the eyes of the world press by incidents like Birmingham is great—yet it is superficial. What really counts is how the citizens of the communities of America respond to such problems.

What we do to control Communist subversion at home, or to combat Communist guerrillas, or to maintain our military strength, or to be first in outer space—none of these things will, in the end, amount to much unless we truly believe that liberty and law are inseparable and that social progress strengthens and enlarges freedom.

It is in fulfilling those beliefs of legal and social

justice that every citizen can and must be a soldier in the cold war—by fighting to improve the soul and not just the face of America.

> The North Carolina Cold War Seminar
> Asheville, North Carolina
> May 17, 1963

Under God and Law

Along Constitution Avenue, just one block from the Department of Justice in Washington, stands a granite pillared building called the National Archives. Enshrined there, under glass, for all to see, are our Constitution and Declaration of Independence. Thousands view them each week.

On the other side of the world, the body of a man named Lenin lies preserved under glass in a tomb in Moscow, and thousands pass through that shrine also.

In 1955, when I visited Moscow, Joseph Stalin was there under glass with Lenin. But now Stalin has been removed.

It would be sort of like us removing the Constitution but leaving the Declaration of Independence.

To me it seems that this is one of the most vivid illustrations of the rule of law versus the rule of man. It is as though each nation had enshrined the source of its law.

The National Archives is today's example of what

Bracton summed up centuries ago with the single phrase: "Not under man, but under God and law."

> University of Virginia Law School
> Charlottesville, Virginia
> May 4, 1963

World Problems and the Individual

... Ours is a time when many things are just too big to be grasped. It is a century which has heaped up enough explosive power to blow up the world. It is a century which has probed into the floor of the sea, which has flung men far into outer space, which now threatens to invade the moon.

When things are done on too vast a scale, the human imagination bogs down. It can no longer visualize such fantastic things and thus looses its grip on their essential reality. Killing one man is murder; killing millions is a statistic. The disclosures of the Eichmann trial remind us all how quickly the world has forgotten the massive horrors which one set of human beings perpetrated against another a short twenty years ago.

Our problems, having grown to the size of the world, if not the solar system, no longer seem our own. Each day we are required to respond to a new crisis created by people whose names we cannot pronounce, in lands of which we have never heard. After a time the capacity to respond begins to flag, and we turn not cheerfully, but almost in despair, to the sports pages and the comics.

And yet I would say to you that the stake is just as personal today as it was a century ago, the obligation just as personal, the capacity to affect the course of history just as great. What we require is not the self-indulgence of resignation from the world but the hard effort to work out new ways of fulfilling our personal concern and our personal responsibility.

> Joint Defense Appeal of the American Jewish Committee and the Anti-Defamation League of the B'nai B'rith
> Chicago, Illinois
> June 21, 1961

Credos

I believe that, as long as there is plenty, poverty is evil. Government belongs wherever evil needs an adversary and there are people in distress who cannot help themselves.

I believe that, as long as the instruments of peace are available, war is madness. Government must be strong wherever madness threatens the peace.

I believe that, as long as most men are honest, corruption is twice vicious. It hurts men and it undermines their fundamental rights. We must be doubly wary with private and public vigilance.

I believe that, as long as a single man may try, any unjustifiable barrier against his efforts is a barrier against mankind. A government that can destroy such a barrier without erecting any others in the process is a good force. A government too weak for that is not only a waste but an evil because it holds out for false hope.

"I Remember, I Believe"
The Pursuit of Justice

Two

TOWARD A BETTER AMERICA

The Urban Dilemma

The plight of the cities—the physical decay and human despair that pervades them—is the great internal problem of the American nation, a challenge which must be met. The peculiar genius of America has been its ability, in the face of such challenges, to summon all our resources of mind and body, to focus these resources and our attention and effort, in whatever amount is necessary, to solve the deepest and most resistant problems. That is the commitment and the spirit required in our cities today.

> Buffalo Model City Conference
> Buffalo, New York
> January 20, 1967

Even as the drive toward bigness, concentration, the city has reached heights never before dreamt of in the past, we have come suddenly to realize how heavy a price we have paid: in overcrowding and pollution of the atmosphere, and impersonality; in growth of organizations, particularly government, so large and powerful that individual effort and importance seem lost; and in loss of the values of nature and community and local diversity that found their nurture in the smaller towns and rural areas of America. And we can see, as we enter the last third of the twentieth century, that the price has been too high. Bigness, loss of community, organizations and society grown far past the human scale—these are the besetting sins of the twentieth century, which threaten to paralyze our very capacity to act, or our ability to preserve the traditions and values of our past in a time of swirling, constant change.

> Worthington, Minnesota
> September 17, 1966

The cities are the nerve system of economic life for the entire nation and for much of the world.

And each of our cities is now the seat of nearly all the problems of American life: poverty and race hatred, interrupted education and stunted lives, and the other ills of the new urban nation—congestion and filth, danger and purposelessness—which afflict all but the very rich and the very lucky.

To speak of the urban condition, therefore, is to speak of the condition of American life. To improve the cities means to improve the life of the American people.

> Statement Before the Senate Subcommittee
> on Executive Reorganization
> August 15, 1966

Both cause and consequence of all the rest [of the cities' problems] is the destruction of the sense, and often the fact, of community, of human dialogue—the thousand invisible strands of common experience and purpose, affection and respect, which tie men to their fellows. It is expressed in such words as community, neighborhood, civic pride, friendship. It provides the life-sustaining force of human warmth and security among others, and a sense of one's own human significance in the accepted association and companionship of others.

We all share things as fellow citizens, fellow members of the American nation.

As important as that sharing is, nations or great cities are too huge to provide the values of community. Community demands a place where people can see and know each other, where children can play and adults work together and join in the pleasures and responsibilities of the place where they live. The whole history of the human race, until today, has been the history of community. Yet this is disappearing—and disappearing at a time when its sustaining strength is badly needed.

> Statement Before the Senate Subcommittee
> on Executive Reorganization
> August 15, 1966

. . . The life lived by the poor in our great urban centers: a life where arrest is common; where "numbers" and narcotics are facts of teen-age life; a world of overburdened parents and children too soon robbed of security, of innocence, of childhood itself. It is a world, above all, of alienation—of lack of communication which threatens to make permanent that sullen second society—that Other America—of which perceptive writers have warned us this past decade.

The tragedy in all of this can be counted in many

ways. It can, of course, be counted in terms of crime, of blighted lives, of subsistence poverty, of broken homes, of malnutrition and disease, and of possibilities and promise unfulfilled. But it is more than a present loss: It is a dark danger to the future. We hear the ticking of a clock—the onrush of ever-greater violence, toward the time of despair, of senseless lashing out with bricks or guns in search of illusory release.

We can count the cost in other ways—in its damage to the sense of community, in ruthless slashing of the thousands of invisible strands which bind man to his fellows, the obliteration—in short—of those shared experiences which, taken together, constitute education for us as individuals and as a people.

> Dedication of Mount Providence Junior College
> Baltimore, Maryland
> September 12, 1966

Francis Bacon tells us that "hope is a good breakfast but a lean supper." In these last five years, we have asked the people of our urban ghettos to the breakfast of hope; but the supper of fulfillment we eat without them.

Breakfast has long been eaten, and hunger walks the streets.

It is time to make room at the table.

> New York Pre-White House Conference
> on Civil Rights
> May 11, 1966

We must attempt . . . to bring worth to individual effort and responsibility. Therefore, every step we take to make our rural areas more attractive and viable—participating in the economy, giving their children the finest possible education, affording their citizens the stimulus and excitement of thought and learning and entertainment—every such step is a gain for all America. For it was Athens, the very mother of cities, which showed us that greatness does not require size—even as others have shown us that size does not necessarily bring greatness.

> Worthington, Minnesota
> September 17, 1966

. . . The time has come to stem the flow to the cities—to prevent their further sprawling over the landscape, their further oppression of men's souls. The time has come when we must actively fight bigness and overconcentration—and seek instead to bring the engines of government, of technology, of the economy, fully under the control of our citizens, to recapture and reinforce the values of a more human time and place.

> Worthington, Minnesota
> September 17, 1966

The people of any ghetto area in which you begin a model neighborhood effort will not and should not have to follow blindly the leadership or accept the direction and control of outsiders—whether from government, or private industry, or foundations. If there is to be any action, any true progress in a neighborhood, that neighborhood itself must be involved in what happens—in the success or failure of any program.

As I sat at the recent hearings on the Cities, I heard witness after witness describe the same indispensable element in any program to help the poor of our cities—whether it be a program to help individuals make ends meet a little more easily or a program to rebuild an entire neighborhood. That element is the self-respect, the self-esteem, the dignity of the individual.

> Buffalo Model City Conference
> Buffalo, New York
> January 20, 1967

Racial Problems

Those of us who are white can only dimly guess at what the pain of racial discrimination must be—what it must be like to be turned away from a public place or made to use only a segregated portion of that place, for no reason other than the color of one's skin.

Prostitutes, criminals, Communist and fascist conspirators—these people are free to go to the movies and to choose their own seats, as long as they are white.

How can a Negro father explain this intolerable situation to his children? And how can the children be expected to grow up with any sense of pride in being Americans?

> Annual Convention of the Theatre Owners
> of America
> Americana Hotel
> New York, New York
> October 28, 1963

If any man claims the Negro should be content or satisfied, let him say he would willingly change the color of his skin and go live in the Negro section of a large city. Then, and only then, has he a right to such a claim.

> Berkeley Campus
> University of California
> October 22, 1966

The great challenge before us is what you have gathered to consider: the revolution within our gates, the struggle of Negro Americans for full equality and freedom.

That revolution has now entered a new stage, one that is at once more hopeful and more difficult, more important and more painful. It is the effort to enforce newly won rights and give them content. . . .

This will not be achieved by a law or a lawsuit, by a single program, or in a single year. It means overcoming the scarred heritage of centuries of oppression, poor education, and the many obstacles to fruitful employment. It means dissolving ghettos—the physical ghettos of our big cities and those ghettos of the mind which separate white from black with hatred and ignorance, fear and mistrust. It means a revolution which has spread from the Deep South to the cities of the North—to every place, in fact, where black Americans seek to leap the gulf dividing them from the city of promise.

Some among us say the Negro has made great progress—which is true—and that he should be satisfied and patient—which is neither true nor realistic. In the past twenty years we have witnessed a revolution of rising expectations in almost every continent. That revolution has spread to the Negro nation confined within our own. Men without hope, resigned to despair and oppression, do not make revolutions. It is when expectation replaces submission, when despair is touched with the awareness of possibility, that the forces of human desire and the passion for justice are unlocked.

For the American Negro that time has come. Courts and congresses and Presidents, in the name of the country, have said that the color of a man's skin shall no longer be a bar to the right to vote, or learn, or work, or enter a public place. We have held out the promise that color shall no longer stand in the way of achievement or personal fulfillment or keep a man from sharing in the affairs of the country. We have unveiled the prospect of full participation in American society, while television, radio, and newspapers bring to every Negro home the knowledge of how rewarding such participation can be. With so bountiful a promise, how much greater must be the frustration and the fury of the Negro—especially the young Negro—who, desperately wanting to believe—and half-believing—finds himself confined in the slums, unable to get an education and a job, confronted by the open prejudice and subtle hostilities of a white world, and seemingly powerless to change his condition or shape his future. For him the progress of the past can count for little against the crushing awareness that his hopes for the future are beyond his reach for reasons which have little to do with justice or his worth as a man. Occasionally broken hope and a deeply felt futility erupt in violence and extreme statements and doctrines. If we deny a man his place in the larger community, then he may turn inward to find his manhood and identity, rejecting those he feels have rejected him. Therefore, far more impressive than the violence of a few is the fact that the overwhelming majority of American Negroes retain their faith in the good will of the nation and the possibilities of peaceful progress within the ordered framework of American politics and life.

> Berkeley Campus
> University of California
> October 22, 1966

Since the dawn of their freedom a century ago, Negro Americans have been advised to "cast down your bucket where you are." But those who offered this advice too often did not bother to look at whether its recipient was standing by a river of opportunity—or in the midst of a desert, from which his bucket could bring back only the sand of poverty and ignorance and want.

Negro Americans have been told to cast down their buckets in search of education. But equal education has not been allowed them—and even today a Negro college graduate can expect to earn less in his lifetime than a white man whose education stopped after the eighth grade.

Negro Americans have been told to cast down their buckets for work. But even now, in the midst of the longest period of sustained expansion in our history, Negro unemployment continues at over twice the white rate; Negroes, as a whole, continue to be paid less than whites for equivalent work; and whole generations of Negro youth have grown up without the chance to learn what work is and what rewards it can bring.

And Negro Americans have been told to cast down their buckets to find and adopt the standards of our society. But our "welfare" programs have too often destroyed families and penalized thrift; our law enforcement has too often stopped short of protecting Negroes from those—white and black—who have preyed on them, in their homes and on their jobs and in the streets; and sometimes we have not even helped them remove the garbage from their neighborhoods.

The time for all this to change is now—just as it has been time to change since the first Negro stepped off the first slave ship onto American soil.

> Second [Manhattan] Borough President's
> Conference of Community Leaders
> on the Revitalization of
> Harlem-East Harlem Community
> New York, New York
> January 21, 1966

The problem that is Watts—and Harlem and Bedford-Stuyvesant and South Chicago and North Philadelphia—is not one that will yield to laws protecting legal rights.

It is the kind of problem that will yield only to other kinds of fundamental change—to the forces created by better education and better housing and better job opportunities.

And it will yield only when the people of the ghetto acquire and wisely exercise political power in the community, only when they are able to establish meaningful communication with a society from which they have been excluded up to now.

The American Negro—already a nation apart for 300 years—is now physically separated from the rest of society by a situation of segregation unparalleled in our country's history. In the great urban areas, he lives in a vast slum where from his birth to his death he enjoys all the privileges of second-class citizenship. Whatever the issue—be it job opportunities, educational facilities, housing, parks, or health care—he comes off second best. . . .

The Negro's frustration about these conditions and

about the massive indifference with which the rest of society had reacted to them was what boiled to the surface in Watts.

The question now is whether we really *did* learn anything from Watts—and from Rochester and Harlem and North Philadelphia.

> WGHO Human Relations Dinner
> Kerhonkson, New York
> April 19, 1966

In the last few months, almost every major city has seen terrible outbreaks of violence—of senseless, terrible rioting, police forces of a dozen major cities unable to cope unaided with it. Who are the rioters? Where do they come from, why do they riot? . . . The McCone Commission found that the riots were caused, more than anything else, by the terrible frustration and alienation of the young Negroes of the impoverished ghetto. The typical rioter was 17, from a fatherless home, unemployed, out of school, without any hope for the future—the typical rioter, the typical dropout, the typical Armed Forces rejectee.

Do we realize that there are, in our major cities, over 500,000 such youth? Can we comprehend that hundreds of thousands more are literally lost to our sight—that they are uncounted by the census, unseen by the unemployment statistics, not on the school rolls, simply drifting about the cities waiting for an explosion to happen—or to make that explosion happen? Seventeen percent of all Negro teen-agers are uncounted by the census—indeed, even in the prime working-age group of 30-34, 13 percent are uncounted. Our society now has no use, no function, for these people. Employers do not hire them; the schools have no place for them; the Army rejects them. They are for all the world like so many starlings or spent matches: there but unseen—until, on occasion, they riot. We all see them then.

> October 3, 1966

Let us, as a beginning, stop thinking of the people of Harlem—the unemployed, the dropouts, those on welfare, and those who work for less than the minimum wage—as liabilities, idle hands for whom some sort of occupation must be found. Let us think of them instead as a valuable resource, as people whose work can make a significant contribution to themselves, their families, and the nation.

> Second [Manhattan] Borough President's
> Conference of Community Leaders
> on the Revitilization
> of Harlem-East Harlem Community
> New York, New York
> January 21, 1966

In Washington, D.C. . . . one small group has shown that it is possible to buy slum tenements, to put them in acceptable repair, and—using the labor of the tenants and of volunteers—to do so without raising rents. This is no easy task, but it is possible. Yet how many of us have organized groups to do this work? How many civil rights organizations or poverty programs have attempted to use available funds to such ends?

The answer is too few.

I do not mean to denigrate the value of protest. Protest for redress of just grievances is the right and the duty of every citizen in a free society. But protest must not be allowed to distract our attention from the job at hand—nor may the need of protest be used as an excuse for our own inaction.

> Second [Manhattan] Borough President's
> Conference of Community Leaders
> on the Revitilization of
> Harlem-East Harlem Community
> New York, New York
> January 21, 1966

The War on Poverty

The War on Poverty is a commitment to the principle that every American shall have the same opportunities to make a life for himself and for his own children—and the same opportunity to share in the government of his city and state and country, the same opportunity to share in the great enterprises of American public life....

This is the legislation—this is the public declaration—that the poor of America are not ignored, not forgotten, that we are willing to see them and hear them and act with them to help them help themselves to be active and productive citizens, and not passive recipients of whatever is left over from our riches.

> October 3, 1966

What we have purchased so far in the war against poverty is new hope for thousands of teen-agers who were on the brink of dropping out of our society, as well as out of school. We have brought a chance for hundreds of thousands of underprivileged children through preschool training in [Operation] Headstart. And we have made available resources to every community that wants to build new bridges of communication to their citizens whom poverty has left without a voice and without a dream. Talking isn't enough. But it is a beginning. We might do better than turning our backs in embarrassed anger when spokesmen for the poor blast the social structure that has left them out. We might listen to them. In the process, we will learn, and they will learn—and out of that simple courtesy, plans and dreams for better communities for everyone may well come to pass.

> WGHO Human Relations Dinner
> Kerhonkson, New York
> April 19, 1966

Let us consider . . . the other items, the other programs, on which the executive branch and we, in the Congress, have thought it worthwhile to spend money.

I cite these examples not to say that they are necessarily wasteful, that they should be abandoned. Many of them I have voted for, and will continue to support. What I do cite them for is to show how meager in comparison is the sum we propose—as a nation—to spend on the key to our future: the elimination of the inequalities of poverty. . . .

—$180 million for the development of a supersonic transport for an aviation industry which had a net profit, in 1965, of over $366 million;

—$50 million to subsidize the construction of airports;
—$82 million for water recreation areas;
—$92 million for highway beautification;
—$3.9 billion for interstate highways. . . .

The poor, those in greatest need, do not generally water-ski, nor do they use airports, and they are less concerned with a highway's smoothness than with whether there is a job waiting at the end of it. We, the fortunate, are providing for our own needs and the needs of our children and our hopes for the future. But we have a greater responsibility to provide for those who cannot help themselves unless we help them do it.

October 3, 1966

In large part . . . responsibilities of personal effort are responsibilities to the poor.

We know our rights. We know when those rights are abridged. And we know how to redress our grievances. But the poor often do not have the tools to protect their interests in a complex world.

The poor are often cheated in the education they receive, in the housing they live in, in the job opportunities available to them. . . .

So if we are to succeed in the process of neighborhood development for the future, we must help to develop neighborhoods—not just for ourselves, but also for those who cannot speak for themselves, who do not know what claims to present.

Neighborhood Preservations and
Renewal Conference
University Heights Campus
New York University
New York, New York
April 2, 1966

The poor have spoken with a thousand voices and in the process have not been understood.

But the poor have spoken. That is a crucial step forward. And they have been heard. And that is an essential success if the country is going to achieve any fundamental social progress.

> WGHO Human Relations Dinner
> Kerhonkson, New York
> April 19, 1966

Education

Education is the key to the jobs of the future.

Education is the key to preserving individual capacity to act, to provide for oneself without dependence on government.

And education, in the last analysis, is the key to understanding the world about us—the world of new nations and nuclear weapons, affluence and starvation, war and peace.

> Des Moines, Iowa
> October 9, 1966

I suspect there may always be arguments about what constitutes a higher education, but wise men through the ages have at least been able to agree on its purpose.

Its purpose is not only to discipline and instruct, but above all to *free* the mind—to free it from the darkness, the narrowness, the groundless fears and self-defeating passions of ignorance.

And so perhaps it's not too much to say that what we are celebrating here today is the liberation, the setting free of your minds.

From now on you have earned the right to do your own learning, to develop your own insights and draw your own conclusions, to conduct your own explorations in the life you find around you. Your minds have been freed.

You may sometimes regret it; for a free mind insists on seeking out reality, and reality is often a far more painful matter than the soft and comfortable illusions of the intellectually poor.

But your regret will be nothing compared with your advantage—the measureless advantage you will always have over the vast majority of human beings on this earth.

In the light of a truly freed mind, no prejudice can disguise itself as zeal, no bullying can masquerade as leadership, no pettiness can pose as importance.

The freed mind will never confuse a sentimentality with a true emotion, an act of violence with an act of heroism, a slogan with a cause.

Men and women with freed minds may often be mistaken, but they are seldom fooled. They may be influenced, but they can't be intimidated. They may be perplexed, but they will never be lost.

> Commencement Exercises
> Trinity College
> Washington, D.C.
> June 2, 1963

In the very process of perfecting our means—of attaining greater and greater expertise in our specialized approaches to knowledge—we are all too likely to settle for false and arrogant assumptions of wisdom. And it is this arrogance that gives rise to the confusion of our goals.

"Our finest convictions," said Ortega y Gasset, "are apt to be the most suspect. They mark our limitations and our bounds. Life is a petty thing unless it is moved by the indomitable urge to extend its boundaries."

One of our own great scientists, Robert Oppenheimer, put the same thought a different way when he was asked to define exactly what it was that scientists of his caliber did all day. They sit around, he said, explaining to each other the things they do not know.

I believe that wise men through the ages have always done just that—for surely the end of true learning is not to establish certainties but to achieve humility in the face of the unknowable.

>Italian Congress of Forensic Medicine
>Americana Hotel
>New York, New York
>September 23, 1963

Listen to a student representative, speaking to a meeting of the Board of Regents of the University of California: "We have asked to be heard. You have refused. We have asked for justice. You have called it anarchy. We have asked for freedom. You have called it license. Rather than face the fear and hopelessness you have created, you have called it communistic. You have accused us of failing to use legitimate channels. But you have closed those channels to us. You, and not us, have built a university based on distrust and dishonesty."

It is impossible to mistake the anguish of that voice. There may be many things in that cry, but one of them is surely a protest of individuality—against the university as corporate bureaucracy, against . . . dull sameness. . . .

> Americans for Democratic Action Dinner
> Philadelphia, Pennsylvania
> February 24, 1967

The classic role of the wife and mother as *just* a wife and mother is something that belongs, I believe, to simpler times than ours—and to simpler minds than yours.

The bland gospel of "togetherness," so sweetly and solemnly spread by merchants over the mass media of this country, can no longer be dismissed as a minor irritant in our popular culture.

It has come to reflect a real and present danger: a growing concept of ideal family life as containment within an airtight capsule of coziness and consumership, a bright plastic bastion from which all the range and clamor of the world is shut out—from which reality itself is forever held at bay.

Don't—as those *other* frightening advertisements used to say—don't let this happen to you.

Consider it imperative, for your own and your husband's and, above, all your children's sake—as well as the sake of your countrymen—that you continue to make full and generous use of the mind your education has set free.

If only with part of your time, and only in the region of your own community—you may find yourself able to work effectively against the forces of darkness around you.

> Commencement Exercises
> Trinity College
> Washington, D.C.
> June 2, 1963

We must insist not only on high standards of education for our own children, but also for those who do not know how to assure their children the education they need.

> Neighborhood Preservation and
> Renewal Conference
> University Heights Campus
> New York University
> New York, New York
> April 2, 1966

We must reach out . . . to those who have been passed by in the past—those already out of school, the fathers and mothers of young children, the unemployed, and the abandoned of this entire nation. Here we must recognize that education is not something—and cannot be allowed to be—something which, once interrupted, is over for life. We need new kinds of universities and colleges—able to teach, not only in fine buildings, but in community centers and parks and even in homes—colleges which are no more than groups of people determined that learning shall be brought to all those who need it.

> Dedication of Mount Providence Junior College
> Baltimore, Maryland
> September 12, 1966

We have always operated our schools on the theory that the school system itself was right; if a child failed, it was the child who was at fault. So we put labels on the children who failed. We called them "culturally disadvantaged"—or "retarded"—or perhaps "lazy" or "stupid."

But the results of this policy are that one quarter to one third of our young men cannot meet even the minimal mental qualifications for the armed forces; that over half the graduates of many of our high schools are unequipped for even the most rudimentary jobs; that hundreds of thousands of children waste away in the blankness of institutions.

We can no longer afford this waste. If our present educational methods cannot do better, then they must be changed to fit the students—just as doctors change a treatment which fails to cure a sick patient. We must now regard a student's failure as the school's failure, and as *our* failure—and hold ourselves responsible for our children's shortcomings.

New York State Society of Newspaper Editors
Utica, New York
February 7, 1966

Youth—the Greatest Resource

Whatever their differences with us, whatever the depth of their dissent, it is vital—for us as much as them—that our young feel that change is possible; that they will be heard; that the cruelties and follies and injustices of the world will yield, however grudgingly, to the sweat and sacrifice they are so ready to give. If we cannot help open to them this sense of possibility, we will have only ourselves to blame for the disillusionment that will surely come. And more than disillusionment—danger; for we rely on these young people more than we know: not just in the Peace Corps, though the Peace Corps has done more for our position around the world than all our armed forces and foreign aid; not just in civil rights, though our youth have done more toward a solution of that problem than all the power and panoply of government; we rely on our youth for all our hopes of a better future—and thus, in a real and direct sense, for the very meaning of our own lives.

> Americans for Democratic Action Dinner
> Philadelphia, Pennsylvania
> February 24, 1967

We have it within our power to give to millions of . . . young people a greater chance at a decent life—to now have a major effect on the course of their next thirty or forty years. Millions are without schools—and we can help to build schoolrooms; millions more are without textbooks, or teachers—and we can help to provide textbooks and train teachers; others cannot eat—and we have food.

Clean water, better housing, education and training, a job to look forward to—these things we can help to provide.

And we must.

Opportunities lost to these young people now, as we have found to our sorrow here at home, will be far harder to make up later. But a relatively modest investment can make a difference, in 50 or 100 years, to as much as half the world's people—including our own.

For our legacy—to our children, to the next generation of political leaders in the United States—will be far more than what we leave within our boundaries. Its most important element will be the role and standing of the United States in the world—whether, in short, people will look to this country with hope or with hate, emulation or envy.

Statement
Senate Floor
July 21, 1966

What . . . young people bring to politics . . . is the knowledge that there are no easy answers, no pat solutions, no permanent panaceas, for the challenges we face. We have learned that peace and progress, at home or in the world, are a process—a way of solving problems; and that the essential ingredient of progress is the willingness to face the problems of our day with blunt honesty and forthright courage.

Democratic State Convention
Manchester, New Hampshire
September 23, 1966

You are a generation which is coming of age at one of the rarest moments in history—a time when all around us the old order of things is crumbling and a new world society is painfully struggling to take shape. If you shrink from this struggle and these many difficulties, you will betray the trust which your own position forces upon you. You live in the most privileged nation on earth. You are the most privileged citizens of that privileged nation; for you have been given the opportunity to study and learn, to take your place among the tiny minority of the world's educated men. By coming to this school you have been lifted onto a tiny sunlit island while all around you lies a dark ocean of human misery, injustice, violence and fear. You can use your enormous privilege and opportunity to seek purely private pleasure and gain. But history will judge you—and, as the years pass, you will ultimately judge yourself—on the extent to which you have used your gifts to lighten and enrich the lives of your fellow man. In *your* hands—not with Presidents or leaders—is the future of your world and the fulfillment of the best qualities of your own spirit.

> Berkeley Campus
> University of California
> October 22, 1966

The nonrecognition of individuality—the sense that no one is listening—is . . . pronounced in our politics. Television, newspapers, magazines, are a cascade of words, official statements, policies, explanations and declarations; all flow from the height of government down to the passive citizen; the young must feel, in their efforts to speak back, like solitary salmon trying to breast Grand Coulee Dam. The words which submerge us, all too often, speak the language of a day irrelevant to our young. And the language of politics is too often insincerity. And if we add to the insincerity, and the absence of dialogue, the absurdity of a politics in which a Byron de la Beckwith can declare as a candidate for lieutenant governor of Mississippi, we can understand why so many of our young people have turned from engagement to disengagement.

> Americans for Democratic Action Dinner
> Philadelphia, Pennsylvania
> February 24, 1967

Devoted and intelligent men have worked for generations to improve the well-being of the American people, diminish poverty and injustice, and protect freedom. Yet, even as we honor their accomplishments, we know that our own problems will not yield to the ideas and programs on which past achievement has been built. Ideas are often more confining—more difficult to discard—in their success than in their failure. Yet we must cast aside many tested concepts in the face of challenges whose nature and dimension are more complex and towering than any before. For this we must look to your [younger] generation, a generation which feels most intensely the agony and bewilderment of the modern age and which is not bound to old ways of thought.

> Berkeley Campus
> University of California
> October 22, 1966

Never again will politics be reserved for the comfortable and the fortunate and the self-seeking. American politics has become, as John Buchan called it, "the greatest, the most honorable adventure." Thousands of young men and women serve in the Peace Corps, in isolated villages and city slums all over the globe. . . . VISTA volunteers, workers for civil rights, young government servants and candidates for Congress—these are the new shape of America's leadership. We have learned, as President Kennedy pledged we would, to judge a man's rank by the size of the job he does—and not by his staff, his budget, or his previous reputation. We give to the young people of America only the opportunity to serve—and they respond with a spirit and dedication which truly lit the world.

> Democratic State Convention
> Manchester, New Hampshire
> September 23, 1966

Racial injustice and poverty, ignorance and hope for world peace are to be found in the streets of New York and Chicago and Los Angeles, as well as in the towns and farmlands of Mississippi.

You have no problem the nation does not have. You share no hope that is not shared by your fellow students and young people across this country. You carry no burden that they, too, do not carry.

This is the reality of the New South. This is the meaning of the modern Southern Revolution, and the chance not only to remedy the mistakes which all of us have made in the past, but to transcend them. Your generation has the chance to serve not only your state, but to take up the troubling burdens of a great nation with global responsibilities. Your generation—*this* generation—cannot afford to waste its substance and its hope in the struggles of the past, when beyond these walls is a world to be helped, and improved, and made safe for the welfare of mankind.

> Law School Forum
> University of Mississippi
> March 18, 1966

The Law

. . . In his proclamation urging us to observe this day, the President emphasized two thoughts. He pointed out that, to remain free, the people must "cherish their freedoms, understand the responsibilities they entail, and nurture the will to preserve them." He then went on to point out that "law is the strongest link between man and freedom."

I wonder in how many countries of the world people think of law as the "link between man and freedom." We know that in many, law is the instrument of tyranny, and people think of law as little more than the will of the state, or the party—not of the people.

And we know too that throughout the long history of mankind, man has had to struggle to create a system of law and of government in which fundamental freedoms would be linked with the enforcement of justice. We know that we cannot live together without rules which tell us what is right and what is wrong, what is permitted and what is prohibited. We know that it is law which enables men to live together, that creates order out of chaos. We know that the law is the glue that holds civilization together.

And we know if one man's rights are denied, the rights of all are endangered. In our country the courts have a most important role in safeguarding these rights. The decisions of the courts, however much we might disagree with them, in the final analysis, must be followed and respected. If we disagree with a court decision and thereafter irresponsibly assail the court and defy its rulings, we challenge the foundations of our society.

. . . Respect for the law—in essence, that is the meaning of Law Day, and every day must be Law Day, or else our society will collapse.

                Law Day Exercises
                University of Georgia Law School
                May 6, 1961

This may be the generation of rising expectations throughout the world. It may be the time when millions of people are released from the chains of ignorance, poverty, and disease which have bound them for centuries.

But it is also the age of nails in the street and the plastic bomb; it is the age of arson, sabotage, kidnappings, and murder for political purposes; it is the age of hit-and-run terrorist activities coordinated on a global scale.

And there is an inherent contradiction between these two conditions. People cannot achieve peace and security, cannot even insure their own personal safety, except under the rule of law.

Only under a government which is an expression of their own will, administered with stability and strength, can they achieve these goals. They cannot do it in chaos.

> Graduation Ceremonies
> International Police Academy
> Washington, D.C.
> February 28, 1964

In 1789 in Hartford, Connecticut, the skies at noon turned one day from blue to gray, and by mid-afternoon the city had darkened over so that, in that religious age, men fell on their knees and begged a final blessing before the end came.

The Connecticut House of Representatives was in session, and many of the members clamored for an immediate adjournment. The Speaker of the House, one Colonel Davenport, came to his feet, and he silenced the din with these words:

"The Day of Judgement is either approaching or it is not. If it is not, there is no cause for adjournment. If it is, I choose to be found doing my duty. I wish, therefore, that candles be brought."

I hope all of you will bring candles to help light our Country's Way.

> University of Virginia Law School
> Charlottesville, Virginia
> May 4, 1963

Civic Responsibility

. . . The laws themselves, of course, while enabling the federal government to do a better job, will not make the final difference. That must come from the extra effort now being made by all the federal law enforcement agencies and many local police officials, and from the support which this effort gets from the American people themselves.

The dishonesty of the gambling operations, the degradation of the narcotic and white-slave traffic are bad enough, but what really concerns me is the great wealth of the racketeers and the power that goes with it—the power to corrupt police and public officials, and, in some instances, gain political control of an area.

The fundamental strength of our democracy, which is based on respect for the law, is at stake.

Individual citizens, by working to elect honest public officials and raise policemen's pay, can make a major difference in this matter. But in the last analysis it depends on the business executive, the factory worker, and the housewife, who have been financing big-time crime with their two-dollar bets and their ten-cent wagers. If they would stop patronizing the illegal bookie, the numbers runner, and the sports-pool operator, they could take the profit out of gambling and bring organized crime down to size quicker than all the combined efforts of the federal and local law-enforcement agencies.

> "The Baleful Influence of Gambling:
> From The Two-Dollar Bet to Narcotics"
> *The Atlantic Monthly*
> April 1, 1962

The spirit of our democracy is that we live together by the rule of law; that we constantly seek the truth; that we speak out when we disagree, and we speak up for unpopular causes; that our government exists for the people and not the people existing for the government.

Our greatest strength and vitality lies in our ability to handle our own affairs in our own communities. Thus, we not only need your patriotic support, but we need your full participation in the affairs of your cities and your states.

> National Commanders' Dinner
> American Legion Convention
> Las Vegas, Nevada
> October 9, 1962

The danger . . . of the extreme Left or Right, is not that they will take control of the American Govern-

Photoreporters (Santi Visalli)

Pictorial

Wide World

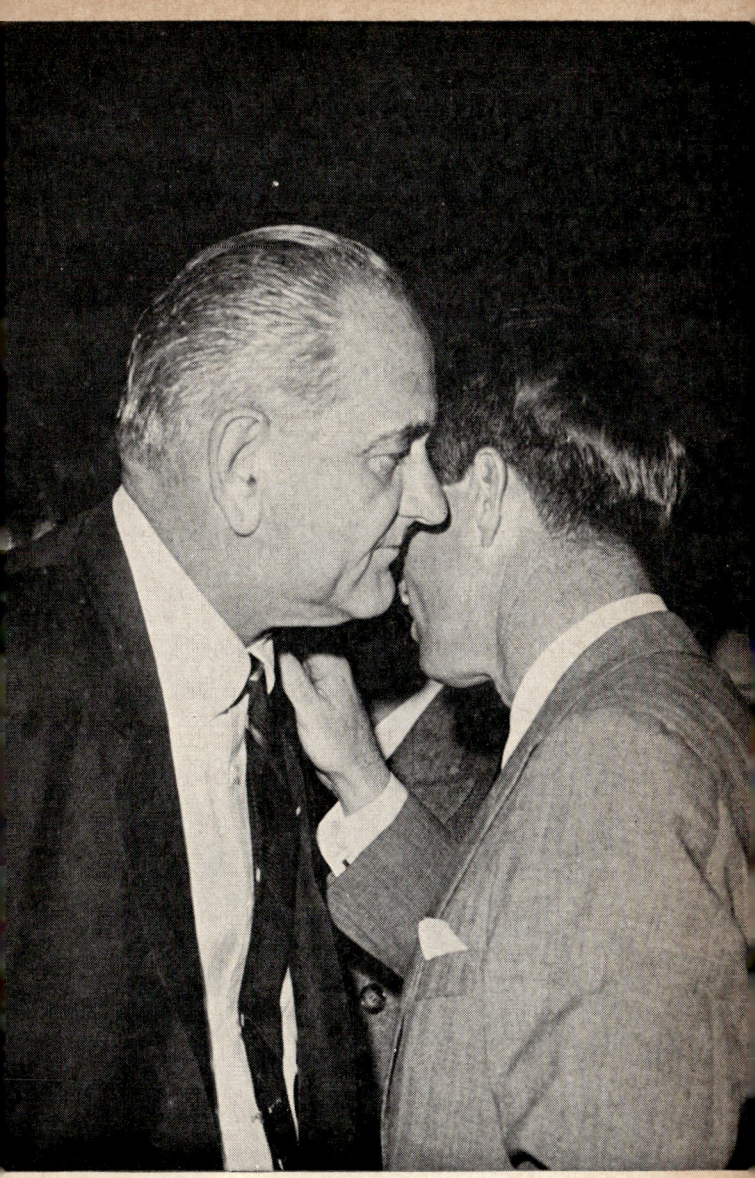

U.P.I.

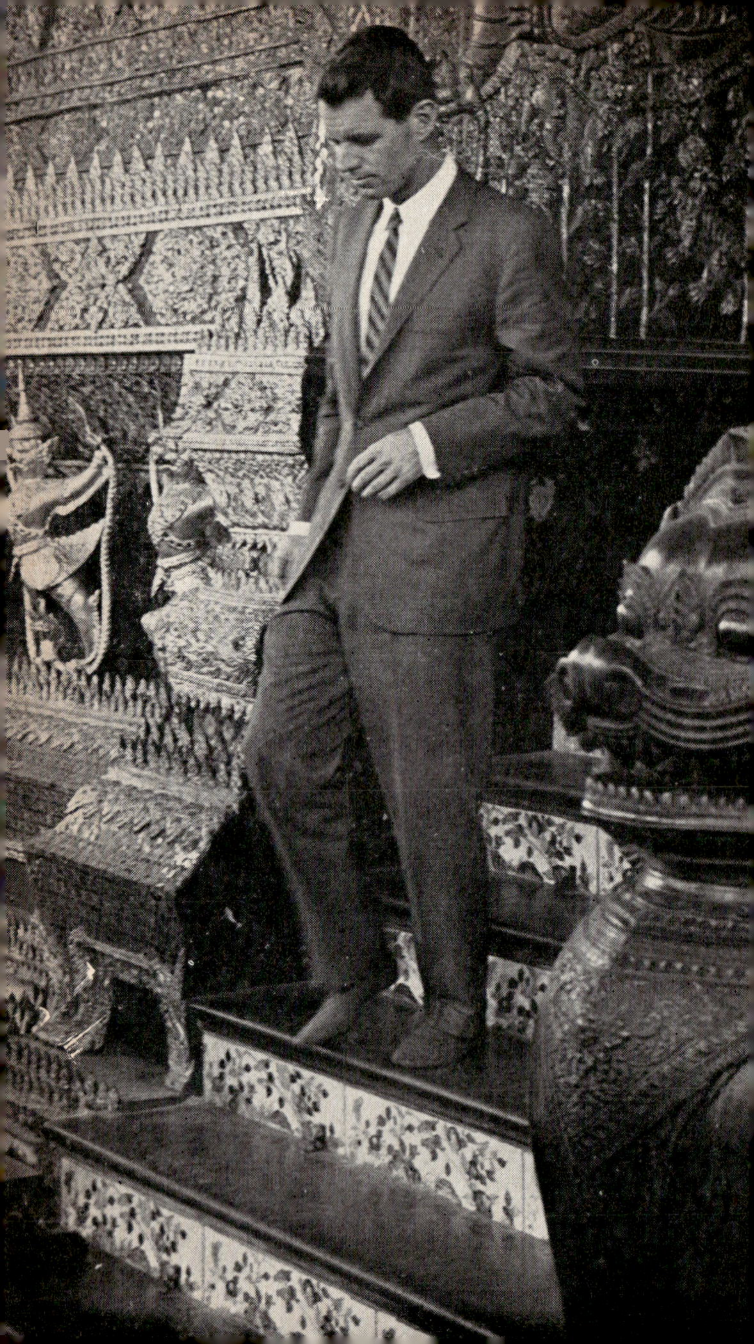

Pictorial

Left: Pictorial

Photoreporters

U. P. I.

Pictorial

Photoreporters

The New York Times (Arthur Brower)

Wide World

Photoreporters

Match from Pictorial

George Tames

U. P. I.

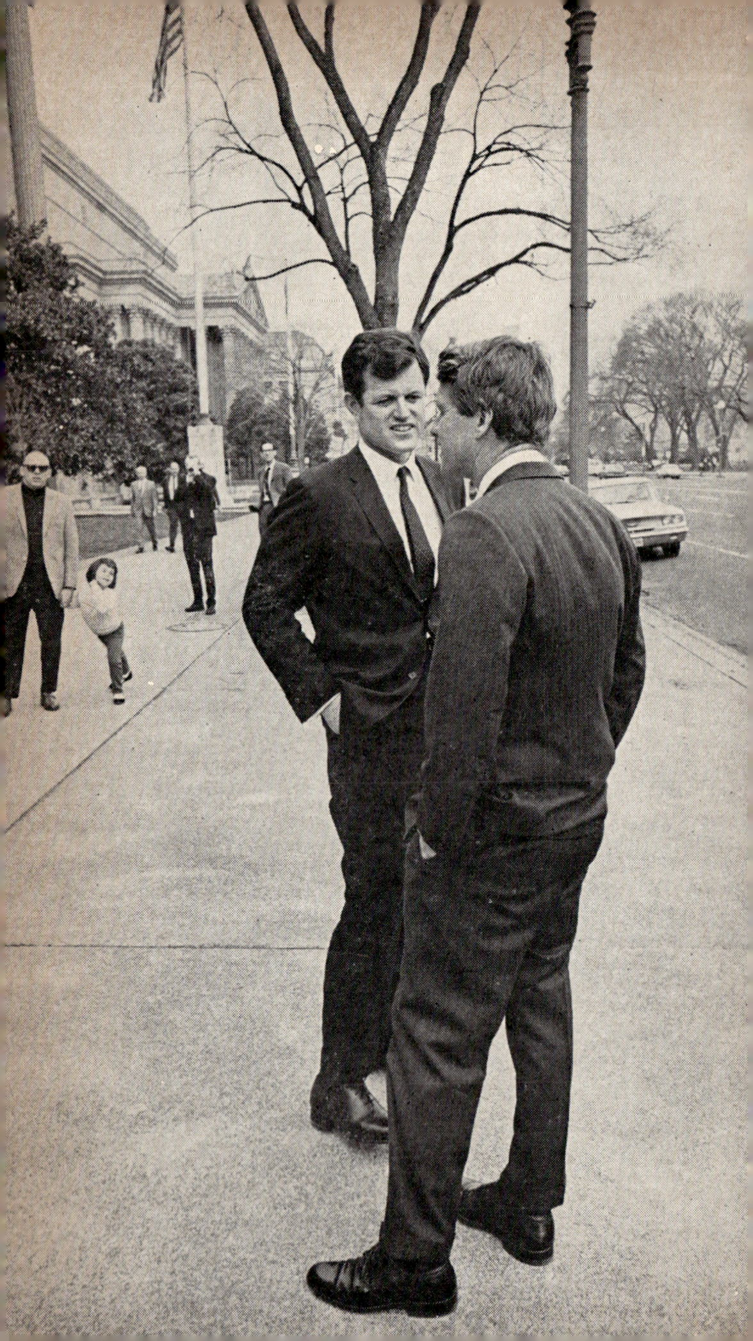

Left: The New York Times (George Tames) Photoreporters

Wide World

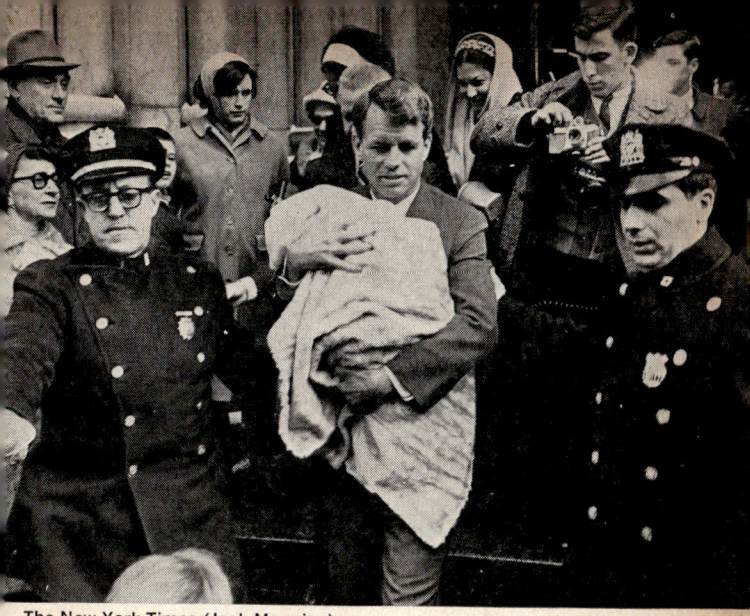

The New York Times (Jack Manning)

The New York Times (George Tames)

U.P.I.

ment. In time, the consensus of good sense which characterizes our political system will digest and discard frozen views and impossible programs. But there is a *short-term* danger from such voices. If they cause enough confusion, stir enough irrational fear, and attract enough political allies, they can restrict and inhibit a President's freedom to take maximum advantage of the openings which the future may present.

The answer to these voices cannot simply be reason, for they speak irrationally. The answer cannot come merely from government, no matter how conscientious or judicious. The answer must come from within the American democracy. It must come from an informed national consensus which can recognize futile fervor and simple solutions for what they are and reject them quickly.

Ultimately, America's answer to the intolerant man is diversity—the very diversity which our heritage of religious freedom has inspired. . . .

Many voices and many views have combined into an American consensus, and it has been a consensus of good sense. "In the multitude of counselors there is safety," says the Bible, and so it is with American democracy. Tolerance is an expression of trust in that consensus, and each new enlargement of tolerance is an enlargement of democracy.

"Extremism, Left and Right"
The Pursuit of Justice

It rests with all of us to take care that all who do rise to power are men and women who hold no interest higher than that of maintaining the system itself.

It is the essence of responsibility to put the public good ahead of personal gain. This still leaves room for individual goals and for the pursuit of them with energy and intelligence. This of course applies to daily life—to the family—as it does to politics. It simply requires that when they take on positions of high responsibility and enjoy the honors of high office they must be willing to relinquish something in return—their narrow self-interests.

Thus, we have nothing to fear from cooperative organization and authority lodged in government unless we fear individualism itself.

> "I Remember, I Believe"
> *The Pursuit of Justice*

The most any law can do is point the way—the rest is up to the people. Civil rights is not an issue that can be solved by governmental edict—it must be dealt with at the community level, within states, within cities, within neighborhoods—wherever a meeting takes place between persons of light and dark skin.

A great deal of hard and conscientious work must be done all over America if we are to fulfill our destiny as a just and democratic nation.

If the disgrace of racial discrimination is to be purged from our land in our time, it won't be a triumph of government alone. It will be a triumph of civil leadership in every American city and town . . . leadership by men responsive to the call for fundamental human justice.

> Annual Convention
> of the Theater Owners of America
> Americana Hotel
> New York, New York
> October 28, 1963

John Adams, writing to Thomas Jefferson in 1821, described free government as "a complicated piece of machinery." Neither had been at the Constitutional Convention of 1787, but both lived to give life and spirit to the product of that meeting. The task of 1787 was to build a new nation from a mosaic of states that boasted of individual sovereignty and honored every detail of their fraternal conflicts. But there was a miracle at Philadelphia—as Catherine Bowen describes it—and, because men were larger than their interests, because they respected vision as well as reality, because they had fought for freedom and knew its price—a nation of boundless opportunity for each of us and all mankind was born.

> Statement Before the Democratic Delegates
> of the Constitutional Convention
> New York, New York
> January 12, 1966

Crime

Saint Thomas Aquinas once said that "freedom is willing obedience to law." There is, of course, no better way to start an argument in a law school than to put forth a simple declarative statement which contains two words like "freedom" and "law." But one of the principal issues facing our society today is just this simple relationship—between law and freedom, justice and order—and the subject matter of your classroom debates is also the center of political debate, the most pressing immediate concern for millions of individual Americans, a matter of literal life and death.

For these people—that is, for the 70 percent of Americans who live in cities—freedom is threatened most of all by the spreading incidence of crime. The most elementary freedoms of all—against arbitrary interference with one's bodily security or property—are in growing jeopardy. As a result, a deepening concern over law enforcement pervades urban society—in the ghettos of Harlem no less than in the row houses of Queens.

> Columbia Law School Forum
> Columbia University
> New York, New York
> January 19, 1967

. . . The problem of crime is greater now than it has been at any time in the past. Ours is a more complex and interdependent society, therefore more vulnerable to disorder; and mobility and instant public communications spread crime—in fact, its example, and its political consequences—more rapidly than ever before.

> Columbia Law School Forum
> Columbia University
> New York, New York
> January 19, 1967

If one thing is clear, it is that organized crime is a national problem. The racketeer is not someone dressed in a black shirt, white tie, and diamond stickpin, whose activities affect only a remote underworld circle. He is more likely to be outfitted in a gray flannel suit, and his influence is more likely to be as far-reaching as that of an important industrialist.

The American public may not see him, but that makes the racketeer's power for evil in our society even greater. Lacking direct confrontation with racketeering, the American citizen is all too likely to fail to see the reason for alarm.

The reason, decidedly, exists. The financial cost of organized crime is not limited to the vast illicit profits of gambling or narcotics. When racketeers bore their way into legitimate business, the cost is borne by the public.

When infiltration is into labor relations, the racketeer's cut is paid by higher wages and high prices—in other words, by the public.

When the racketeer bribes local officials and secures immunity from police action, the price exacted by corrupt law enforcement, incalculable in dollars, is paid, again, by the public.

The Pursuit of Justice
"Free Enterprise in
Organized Crime"

. . . Crime is principally a problem of young people. In 1965, almost three quarters of those arrested for serious crimes were between 13 and 29. Historically, increases in crime in this country have been closely related to increases in the size of the 13 to 29 age group; our recent increases in crime rates are in direct proportion to the "baby boom" of recent years; and, as the youth population continues to grow, we can expect a serious continued growth of crime in the next decade and beyond. Thus, our proposals must be shaped by the problem—by its character as a phenomenon of the teen-ager and the young adult.

> Columbia Law School Forum
> Columbia University
> New York, New York
> January 19, 1967

Crime is not just in the streets. It is in the suburbs too. It is in white-collar offices and business. And it is organized.

Too often there is a tendency to dismiss tax evasion or stock fraud as unimportant, or as the miscalculation of one who was not clever enough to stay within the law. But the public attitudes which condone fixing—of prices or of traffic tickets—are attitudes which undermine respect for law throughout the society.

Crime in the streets is directly related to these attitudes, and especially to public apathy about organized crime. The young man in the ghetto who decides to steal rather than make that extra effort to find work is unquestionably influenced by the success which the numbers runner down the block has had. The bookmaker or the narcotics pusher is all too often the only conspicuous figure of success in the ghetto, the one who has demonstrated how to beat the system and gain wealth and prominence. Similarly, the worker who belongs to a corrupt union, or the businessman who must pay protection to keep his business or his life, are taught every day—as are their children—that our legal system has nothing to offer them. As long as the public cares too little about the racketeers who control the gambling, and the narcotics, and the prostitution that feed upon the poor and the weak, there will be youngsters who see the gangster's way as the model, the path to follow.

> Columbia Law School Forum
> Columbia University
> New York, New York
> January 19, 1967

Crime is a disease that is never totally cured. It exists under socialism as under capitalism, in primitive and advanced cultures—under all political forms. All societies have alienated and disaffected members; and some proportion of men will always prefer to act outside the rules to achieve personal advantage. This does not mean that crime cannot be reduced by reforming society; of course it can. It does mean that it cannot be eliminated, and that law enforcement will always be needed.

> Columbia Law School Forum
> Columbia University
> New York, New York
> January 19, 1967

. . . It is clear that reducing crime involves far more than reform of the law enforcement system. Over the long run it involves the building of a society in which people do not want to and do not feel the need to violate the law—a society where equal opportunity for all is a reality, a society where self-respect and self-esteem are not commodities reserved for the economically advantaged. And that effort in turn requires that we vastly multiply our efforts against poverty, for education, for jobs, for fundamental justice in the economic and social relations between men.

Columbia Law School Forum
Columbia University
New York, New York
January 19, 1967

Everywhere he turns, the young ex-convict finds that the government which has urged him to pursue a normal, law-abiding life is the same government that bars the way to that pursuit. In some states, licensing requirements may prevent the releasee from becoming a barber or an embalmer—to mention only a few of the existing prohibitions. By reason of various state statutes, certain manufacturers cannot employ convicted felons. Other businessmen will not employ them because the state has taken no action to help the ex-convict obtain an employment bond. Public employment remains virtually closed to the releasee. He cannot even qualify for unemployment insurance because he has not earned a sufficient amount of money during the preceding year. And all of this takes no account of the natural barriers that stand in the ex-convict's way because he has had little opportunity for education or job training while he was in prison.

Under these circumstances, the ex-convict must normally turn to friends or to family for assistance. If he is rejected by them, then his next step is a welfare mission on skid row. At any point along the way it may simply be easier for him to return to crime.

This nightmarish world must be changed if we are to prevent the large-scale recurrence of crime.

Columbia Law School Forum
Columbia University
New York, New York
January 19, 1967

Violence

However much the condition of most Negroes must call forth compassion, the violence of a few demand condemnation and action. In the streets of many of our cities, in recent months, we have seen riots and looting and even occasional murder. Still far more disturbing than the chaotic, self-destructive violence of Watts or Oakland are the statements of a very few Negro spokesmen—those who have called for hatred to fight prejudice, racism to meet racism, violence to destroy oppression. Here is the seed of tragedy for black and white alike.

To understand the causes is not to permit the result. No man has the right to wantonly menace the safety and well-being of his neighbors. All citizens have the right to security in the streets of their community—in Birmingham or in Los Angeles. And it is the duty of all public officials to keep the public peace and bring to justice those who violate it.

> Berkeley Campus
> University of California
> October 22, 1966

Why not turn to violence? . . .

How many, watching the faces of Grenada, must have asked again, how long—how long turn the other cheek, how long hold to the counsels of nonviolence?

But the course of violence would be terribly, awfully wrong: not just because hatred and violence are self-defeating—though they are self-defeating, for they strike at the very heart of obedience to law, peaceful process, and political cooperation, which are man's last [and] best hopes for a decent world. . . . The central disease of violence is what it does to all of us—to those who engage in it as much as to those who are its victims.

Cruelty and wanton violence may temporarily relieve a feeling of frustration, a sense of impotence. But the damage of those who perpetrate it—these are the negation of reason and the antithesis of humanity, and they are the besetting sins of the twentieth century.

Surely the world has seen enough, in the last forty years, of violence and hatred. Surely we have seen enough of the attempt to justify present injustice by past slights, or to punish the unjust by making the world more unjust.

We know now that the color of an executioner's robe matters little. And we know in our hearts, even through times of passion and discontent, that to add to the quantity of violence in this country is to burden our own lives, and mortgage our children's souls and the best possibilities of the American future.

>   Berkeley Campus
>   University of California
>   October 22, 1966

Dissent—a Right and a Responsibility

It is not enough to allow dissent. We must demand it. For there is much to dissent from. . . .

Yet we must, as thinking men, distinguish between the right of dissent and the way we choose to exercise that right. It is not enough to justify or explain our actions by the fact that they are legal or constitutionally protected. The Constitution protects wisdom and ignorance, compassion and selfishness alike. But that dissent which consists simply of sporadic and dramatic acts sustained by neither continuing labor or research—that dissent which seeks to demolish while lacking both the desire and direction for rebuilding, that dissent which, contemptuously or out of laziness, casts aside the practical weapons and instruments of change and progress—that kind of dissent is merely self-indulgence. It is satisfying, perhaps to those who make it.

But it will not solve the problems of our society. It will not assist those seriously engaged in the difficult and frustrating work of the nation. And, when it is all over, it will not have brightened or enriched the life of a single portion of humanity in a single part of the globe.

> Berkeley Campus
> University of California
> October 22, 1966

Our Constitution imposes on the Senate the most heavy and grave independent responsibilities. We ourselves owe to the people of 50 States the burden of independent thought and action. . . .

Shall we then debate with force and passion the issues of labor relations and housing and trade—while the great issues of peace and war are allowed to pass in silence? Shall we discuss the standard of living of our constituents—while policies which affect their very existence go undiscussed? To do so would be the gravest departure from our duties as representatives of the people of the American States.

Full and informing debate rests upon moderation and mutual indulgence. Men must seek acceptance of their views through reason, and not through intimidation; through argument, and not through accusation.

We are all patriots here. We are all defenders of freedom. We are all Americans.

To attack the motives of those who express concern about our present course—to challenge their very right to speak freely—is to strike at the foundations of the democratic process which our fellow citizens, even today, are dying in order to protect.

U.S. News & World Report
March 7, 1966

The Press

. . . I do not believe that newspapermen are self-appointed judges of what's right and wrong or what's good or bad. But I believe in and greatly admire those who are competent to seek the truth and inform the people. In my opinion, the newspapers are equal to the courts—and sometimes ahead of the courts—in our system in protecting the people's fundamental rights.

> "Misinformation and Missunderstanding
> About the U.S."
> (Responsibility to get the
> Truth to the People)
> Annual Luncheon of the Associated Press
> New York, New York
> April 23, 1962

. . . There are so many internal problems which the press can help solve, which in the last analysis relate to honest, efficient administration of government—whether it is in a city, county, state or federal agency.

It is virtually impossible for even the most alert administration to be fully aware of all the corruption or laxity that can creep into our government. But an alert press can make a major difference—not only in eliminating wasteful or corrupt practices—but in insuring that justice prevails.

> "Misinformation and Misunderstanding
> About the U.S."
> (Responsibility of Press to get the
> Truth to the People)
> Annual Luncheon of the Associated Press
> New York City, New York
> April 23, 1962

Air Pollution

On a trip to Latin America last year, I saw people in Recife, in the poorest part of Brazil, who ate crabs which lived off the garbage that the people themselves threw in the shallow water near their shabby rooms. And whenever I tell this story to Americans, the reaction is: How sad, how terrible, that such poverty, such underdevelopment, should exist in the world!

But we New Yorkers are in a poor position from which to extend pity. For every year the average New Yorker—old and young, rich and poor, athlete or infirm recluse—breathes in 750 pounds of his own wastes. The fuel which generates our electricity, the gasoline which runs our cars and taxicabs and busses, the four pounds of trash and garbage which each of us gives the city each day, and even the garbage we drop into our apartment-house incinerators—all these are discharged into the air we breathe. And because there are so many of us crowding into this tiny fraction of the United States, a great pall of filthy air blankets the entire metropolitan area—and we all must breathe the same air into which we carelessly spill our refuse.

> New York-New Jersey Metropolitan Area
> Air Pollution Control Conference
> January 4, 1967

... We should not—we cannot—wait for technology to make clean air entirely painless, to be achieved without effort, like a genie waving a magic wand. We will never get anywhere unless we begin now to apply what we do know. Technological progress may reduce costs later; that will be all to the good. But we all pay for air pollution now, every day. Without even counting the cost to human life and health—for these are literally beyond price—it is clear that air pollution costs the people of New York at least $1 billion a year—$70 for every man, woman, and child in the metropolitan area. That cost we pay every day; surely we can invest one tenth of that amount to save ourselves the other nine tenths.

We should, I believe, beware of the pitfalls described by Twain:

> Imagine a man who sets out on a voyage equipped with a pair of spectacles that magnify things to an extraordinary degree. A hair on his hand, a spot on the tablecloth, the shifting of a coat, all will attract his attention; at this rate, he will not go far, he will spend his day taking six steps and will never get out of his room.

We have to get out of the room.

> New York-New Jersey Metropolitan Area
> Air Pollution Control Conference
> January 4, 1967

... We will make our air fit to breathe only if we are all determined that the air will be clean. Democracies, which rely on popular consent, seem often to make the mistake of Faust—who looked only at the pleasure of the passing moment, with no thought to its cost in the future. Our past failures will surely lead us to disaster—as President Johnson has described it, the "reckless devastation" that is "the continued poisoning" of our air.

But I believe there is a new spirit abroad in the land, a new hope that these great problems will yield to the inventive genius and capacity for action of the American nation. Citizens' groups, informed and alert and well-organized, have sprung up spontaneously. Public officials have become newly aware, more ready to act. We can seize and ride that spirit now—or we can let it dissolve in bureaucratic apathy, in endless studies, in refusal to assess the true costs of air pollution against their sources. . . .

> New York-New Jersey Metropolitan Area
> Air Pollution Control Conference
> January 4, 1967

Drug Addiction

. . . Addiction is not a problem that will be solved in any simple way. The addict is a product of a society that has left him behind. Addiction will continue to occur as long as the social conditions which give rise to it exist. Some 75 percent of those addicted to heroin come from the 20 percent of society with the lowest incomes. Until there are enough jobs to go around, until everyone has a decent home and a decent education, until we have uniformly stable and secure family structures—in short, until the world is a much better place than it is now—the mental problems associated with addiction—and addiction itself, in one form or another—will continue to occur.

> Testimony on Narcotics Legislation
> Senate Judiciary Committee
> January 26, 1966

In the fight against narcotics addiction, it is a responsibility to realize that all the treatment facilities that money can buy will do no good unless the addict can be convinced that there is reason for him to try and rehabilitate himself—reason for him to want to rejoin a society that he thinks has no use for him.

> Neighborhood Preservation and Renewal
> Conference
> University Heights Campus
> New York University
> New York, New York
> April 2, 1966

Protecting the Consumer

One original purpose of the regulatory agencies was protection of consumer interests. Yet it increasingly occurs that the consumer's voice before these agencies is drowned out by the competition of one more particularized interest or another. Why shouldn't young people who will be enticed to smoke by cigarette advertising be spoken for when the tobacco interests are heard so clearly? Why shouldn't the users of electricity be heard when giant utilities are spoken for so effectively? Why shouldn't those who borrow from banks be heard as well as the financial institutions themselves? . . . It is not easy to organize the consumers so that their point of view can be consistently and effectively set forth. But a Federal department, specifically charged with that obligation, could give the consumer the voice he needs in the regulatory process.

> Testimony on H.R. 7179 [creation of a
> Department of Consumers]
> House Committee of Government Operations
> New York, New York
> April 29, 1966

I am especially concerned about the protection of the poor. The disadvantages of the poor extend to every contact they have with the world of commerce. The quality of their food is lower, and the prices they pay are often higher; the interest rates they pay are higher; they are more often the victims of the high pressure tactics of deceitful salesmen. And they are the most frequent casualties of the various laws that protect the producing interests of our society: The poor suffer again and again through the entry of default judgements against them, through the repossessing of merchandise, and through misuse of landlord and tenant laws.

> Testimony On H.R. 7179 [creation of a
> Department of Consumers]
> House Committee on Government Operations
> New York, New York
> April 29, 1966

Sports and Athletics

Consider for a moment what we achieve from athletics. First of all, there is the sheer fun of playing—whether it be tennis, swimming, baseball, or football. Beyond that, and the building of a healthy body and the assistance in the formation of a healthy and alert mind, we develop stamina, courage, unselfishness, and —most importantly, perhaps—the will to win.

What a difference these characteristics make in our later lives, no matter what we do—no matter what our vocation might be—even if it be just in small things! You have all seen the small boy watch an older brother or friend hang and drop from a jungle gym and then muster the courage to give it a try himself. What a cry of delight and pride follows. When he makes the drop, he has achieved something that is important in his life, something that is necessary in the making of a man. He holds himself a little straighter. He feels himself a little stronger.

> Address, "Dinner of Champions"
> Astor Hotel
> New York, New York
> October 17, 1961

The world of sports has no religious, racial, or political differences. Athletes, from whatever land they come, speak the same language. The lessons of competition are lessons for life. The athletic arena is the ideal place for our contemporaries to meet.

For this kind of courage, competitiveness, and respect for others that is so evident among our athletes is what is needed so much today by all Americans—by all people who cherish freedom. The problems we face are immense. The challenges are so enormous that they are often difficult to comprehend. But admitting all that, . . . the future for all of us . . . and for our children can be bright and promising.

>Address, "Dinner of Champions"
>Astor Hotel
>New York, New York
>October 17, 1961

Part of the nation's prestige in the Cold War is won in the Olympic Games. In this quadrennial conflict, the U.S. has skidded steadily for 16 years. The record is there for all the world to see—and to note as proof of a decline in our once-acknowledged national energy.

It doesn't have to be that way. A series of well-organized and well-financed programs—matching or bettering those of other countries—can restore the bright and gleaming Golden Age of Sports which gave us an inner glow of pride and enhanced the picture abroad of a young America bursting with vitality. . . .

It may seem that our downhill trend since the 1948 Games is contradicted by the performances and prospects of the excellent athletes who are trying out for the 1964 U.S. Olympic team. . . . But as outstanding as these men and their fellow competitors are, the fact is that the athletes of other countries are catching up—

and then some—while we have done very little toward developing and promoting proficiency among our young potential athletes or toward encouraging a strong and meaningful athletic program.

Our task is to arouse interest in this problem. Then we need action to develop the great potential that we have in this country and to reverse a trend that we have avoided facing for so long.

> "A Bold Proposal for America Sport"
> *Sports Illustrated*
> July 27, 1964

In too many neighborhoods in the past, the short-term claims of the adults have taken precedence over the long-term claims of our young people and of our future. There isn't much sand-lot baseball anymore—no sand lots.

This is one place where our modern, complacent society could have done better. Playfields can't substitute for a proper parent-child relationship and a secure family life. But recreation areas can be helpful, and we need more of them.

> Address, "Dinner of Champions"
> Astor Hotel
> New York, New York
> October 17, 1961

Suffrage

I urge the abolition of ... [New York State's] literacy test for voting. Whatever justification there once was for such qualifications, it does not exist today. Television and radio communicate to the people without differentiation between the literate and those who, for one reason or another, never acquired the ability to read the written word.

There is no indication whatever that the political life of the thirty states which have no literacy tests has been debased by the universality of the suffrage. And the fact is that the literacy test tends to disenfranchise those who have the greatest stake in the political process. As Lord Acton said:

> "Laws should be adapted to those who have the heaviest stake in the country, for whom misgovernment means not mortified pride or stinted luxuries but want and pain, and degradation and risk to their own lives and to their children's souls."

Keeping from the polling booth those who have the greatest interest in the results of the contest is to me the reverse of good sense.

New York State Joint Legislative
Committee on the Election Law
New York, New York
January 20, 1966

I urge that New York's constitution be amended to lower the voting age to eighteen. I believe our young people have shown that they are mature enough at that age to participate in the process of government. Their record of concern and action for civil rights, and in public affairs generally, is one of which we can all be proud and has proven—if proof was needed—that they would contribute significantly to the quality of American government if they had the franchise. And rewarding their interest and participation in the vote might well have useful effects in encouraging their continued participation later in life.

> New York State Joint Legislative
> Committee on the Election Law
> New York, New York
> January 20, 1966

Medicare—a Realistic View

Medicare fulfilled a dream of a generation's standing, for social progress moves slowly, and statutory reforms often lag behind scientific achievement and popular will....

But Medicare also imposes a great responsibility on us. It summons us to the task of ensuring not only that the cost of medical care is no longer a burden upon those who need but cannot afford it, but that good medical care itself is available. The bright hopes of Medicare can be dashed if we fail to achieve this availability.

What, after all, is the value of offering medical treatment to our aged if there are no doctors available to administer it? What is the value of offering nursing home care to our old people if there are no nursing homes where they can go? What is the value of offering hospital treatment to those aged who are seriously ill if there are no hospital beds waiting for them? The dream quickly becomes a nightmare; the bright promise becomes a dreary broken pledge; the loud trumpets announcing victory slide into a lower key of despair. Unless we, as a nation, are prepared right now to ensure that we have the facilities needed to implement the Medicare legislation, we would almost have been better off to have done nothing. If we are not prepared to move forward, energetically and imaginatively, to build on the blueprint of the Medicare legislation, then we had better be prepared for some very serious problems.

                        Judy Holliday Memorial Dinner
                        American Medical Center
                        Americana Hotel
                        New York, New York
                        May 15, 1966

Automobile Safety

All of us have learned from the advances in aerospace and aviation that we can have car brake systems that "fail safe" and not in a crash; that steering mechanisms can have a back-up system that gives the driver control if the main system fails; that car seats and dashboards can be designed to protect rather than maim or kill.

Failure analysis has been developed into a fine science. . . .

Engineers know from experience when a part will fail; they know by calculation when a system will fail. And, when a system of parts cannot be made sufficiently safe, they design a back-up system that will take over in case of failure.

Americans know that we have the technical knowledge to build these devices—and that they do not need to be prohibitively expensive.

Still, the industry has claimed that the problems of brake failure, tire collapse, and other major failures are beyond their engineering skill.

These same manufacturers are willing to guarantee the reliability of complex missile and space systems they sell to the armed forces.

The contrast is odd indeed.

I submit that there is no lack of engineering ability in the United States today.

Excuses for catastrophic failure . . . are an insult to the professional abilities of all American engineers.

The truth is that engineers are not *asked* to design for safety.

> American Trial Lawyers Association
> Waldorf Astoria
> New York, New York
> February 2, 1966

It will . . . be argued that the cost of the safety features themselves is prohibitive.

But the cost of traffic accidents last year—measured only in insurance payments for death, injury, and damage; in days lost from work; in congestion in the courts and in the hospitals—this cost was 8 billion dollars. . . .

And the human cost is beyond measurement. . . .

Further inaction will be criminal—for it will be with full knowledge that our action can make a difference, that auto deaths can be cut down, that the slaughter on our highways is needless waste.

Present airport runways are often inadequate for high-performance aircraft, and planes sometimes crash as a result.

When military commanders want money to extend these runways, they place the boots of the dead pilots on the conference table before them.

The boots of millions of traffic victims, past and future are on the table before us.

It is time to act.

> American Trial Lawyers Association
> Waldorf Astoria
> New York, New York
> February 2, 1966

Three

FOREIGN AFFAIRS:
A REASONED APPROACH

America's Role in a World Community

There is one thing which Americans have come to understand in these last decades. That is that we cannot hope to realize . . . [our] purposes in isolation from the rest of the world. The turbulence of social change has long since begun to spill across national frontiers. The overriding development of the second half of the twentieth century is the awakening of peoples in Asia and Africa and Latin America—peoples stirring from centuries of stagnation, suppression, and dependency. Now they are seeking through national independence the kind of economic and social development which both your country and mine have experienced. These are young nations, trying desperately in the quest for political and social progress to make up for lost centuries.

The resources of the earth and the ingenuity of man can provide abundance for all—so long as we are prepared to recognize the diversity of mankind and the variety of ways in which peoples will seek national fulfillment. This is our vision of the world—a diversity of states, each developing according to its own traditions and its own genius, each solving its economic and political problems in its own manner, and all bound together by a respect for the rights of others, by a loyalty to the world community, and by a faith in the dignity and responsibility of man.

> "The Goals of Government"
> Nihon University
> Tokyo, Japan
> February 6, 1962

We do not stand fast at Berlin just because we are against Communism. We stand at Berlin because we have a positive and progressive vision of the possibilities of free society, because we see freedom as the instrumentality of social progress and social justice; because Communism itself is but the symptom and the consequence of the fundamental evils: ignorance, disease, hunger, and want. Freedom has shown mankind the most effective way to destroy these ancient antagonists.

The free way of life proposes ends, but it does not prescribe means. It assumes that people and nations will often think differently, have the full right to do so; and that diversity is the source of progress. It believes that men advance by discussion, by debate, by trial, and by error.

It believes that the best ideas come not from edict and ideology, but from free inquiry and free experiment; and it regards dissent, not as treason to the state, but as the tested mechanism of social progress. And it knows that diverse nations will find diverse roads to the general goal of political independence and economic growth. It regards the free individual as the source of creativity and believes that it is the role of the state to serve him and not his role to serve the state.

> "Berlin East and West—A Controlled Experiment"
> *The Pursuit of Justice*

We must realize that we cannot put down disorder everywhere in the hemisphere and concentrate, instead, on programs for social improvement which will minimize disorder. It is one thing to send 30,000 troops to an island nation of 3.6 million, of whom a few thousand were under arms in a single major city. It would be something else indeed to attempt the same thing in a country like Brazil, larger than the United States, with a population of 80 million; or Argentina, with 24 million people and vast expanses of plain; or any of the nations of the Andean fastness.

> "The Alliance for Progress: Symbol and Substance"
> Speech in the Senate of the United States
> May 9 and 10, 1966

No matter how brilliantly we build, how generously we pour forth our treasure, how wisely we use our power; if we neglect the reality behind the act, then we will surely fall. Leadership in freedom cannot rest on wealth and power. It depends on fidelity and persistence in those shaping beliefs—democracy, freedom, justice—which men follow from the compulsions of their hearts and not the enslavement of their bodies. We must cope with real dangers, overcome real obstacles, meet real needs; but always in a way which preserves our own allegiance to the principles of the Alliance. Otherwise we will preserve the shadow of progress and security at the expense of the substance of freedom in the New World.

> "The Alliance for Progress: Symbol and Substance"
> Speech in the Senate of the United States
> May 9 and 10, 1966

[In Asia] I have seen men clambering out of stagnation and squalor and demanding to be admitted to the twentieth century.

I have seen a new world beginning to emerge out of centuries of oblivion.

Half of the earth is marching out of the darkness into the sunlight.

It is a stirring experience to watch whole nations struggling to achieve political independence and economic growth.

It is stirring, and it is significant, because the energies released in this great historic movement—let us not mistake this—are going to reshape the world and determine the future of man.

> "The New Frontier and The New Europe"
> Beethoven Hall
> Bonn, Germany
> February 24, 1962

I think that, generally, there should be a greater awareness in this country—and abroad—of all that we do and all that we have done. There's too much concentration on what our faults are and what our problems are.

We go into India and help them because they are being invaded by the Chinese, and the Pakistanis get mad. And we take steps to build the Skybolt missile and then we find that it's not a success, and so it's canceled, and other people get mad.

Everybody gets angry over what we are doing. The kind of effort that we've made over the period of the last 20 years, helping and assisting countries around the world, is something of which we should be extremely proud. I don't think we need apologize for our record.

I also don't think we have to accept criticisms that are continuously leveled at us from other countries because we don't do exactly as they desire. They are interested in their countries, and, frequently, that is their sole interest. We have other interests, other responsibilities, and I don't think we have to make any apology for what we have done, what we have contributed—the effort and the sacrifice that we make.

U.S. News & World Report
January 28, 1963

A Purpose Beyond Our Shores

... Even during periods of weakness and division we have been a country with a purpose beyond our shores. How much more effectively can we pursue that purpose now that we are strong and united! There is no question of our capacity; the only question is whether success and riches and power have eroded the energy and daring needed to lead a revolution in the condition of the world.

Have our triumphs and conquests erased the visions which adversity, struggle, and danger could not dim?

I do not think so. Everywhere I travel I meet a generation anxious to share, not only in elevating their own society, but in taking part in the revolution now reshaping their world.

> Columbus Day Dinner
> Waldorf Astoria Hotel
> New York, New York
> October 11, 1966

In troubled times there is always a temptation to grow one's own hedge and cultivate one's own garden. For either the United States or Europe to succumb to such a temptation would be unworthy of our past—and unfaithful to our future.

We cannot—you in Europe and we in the United States—become fortresses within ourselves, dealing with and helping only one another.

If we do so we will not be meeting our responsibilities to the rest of mankind—and very likely we will be spelling our own destruction.

> "The New Frontier and the New Europe"
> Beethoven Hall
> Bonn, Germany
> February 24, 1962

Americans who go abroad should do so with a sense of responsibility for providing full and factual answers.

It is not enough simply to send thousands of students abroad and believe that, because they are nice young boys and girls who "mix," this will be sufficient. If they go to Germany and don't know anything about the Berlin wall; if they go to Indonesia and don't know about the West New Guinea problem; if they go to African countries and don't know what we are trying to accomplish at home in the field of racial discrimination; if they are good-looking, pleasant, eager—and uninformed—we are just not going to get the job done. It would be better for them to stay home.

Saturday Review
February 16, 1963

Students abroad must discuss our problems intelligently, admit our problems, and must say what we are trying to do about them. This is, after all, one of our country's great strengths—we admit our problems, but we try to take action to solve them and face up to our responsibilities.

The need is to be candid about our problems and to be informed on what we're doing about them. Unlike the highly trained Communist infiltrators and propagandists, we have no "party line" in this country. Nor is there a need of one. The facts—as opposed to the stereotypes exploited by our adversaries—will speak for themselves.

Saturday Review
February 16, 1963

Peace

We must . . . help find a way to dissolve the attitudes which permit men to indulge those passions and ambitions which keep the world in constant conflict and which threaten the survival of all of us. There have been some seventy wars since the end of World War II, and we have made virtually no progress in reducing the capacity for nuclear destruction. In fact it is constantly increasing. We cannot do this by ourselves. Yet we *can* show increased understanding for the fears and suspicions of others and act on the knowledge that it is worthwhile to take occasional risks in the name of peace.

> Columbus Day Dinner
> Waldorf Astoria Hotel
> New York, New York
> October 11, 1966

The peace we seek [is not] simply the absence of armed conflict or hostile division. It is the creation among nations of a web of unity, woven from the strands of economic interdependence, political cooperation, and a mounting flow of people and ideas.

> Columbus Day Dinner

Waldorf Astoria Hotel
New York, New York
October 11, 1966

Nuclear Restraint

Change—swirling, dizzying, unstoppable change—has made us all mariners on uncharted seas. The world has changed more, in the last 50 years, than it changed in the three thousand years before this century. . . .

Once we sought telescopes to see the planets; now we build ships to reach them.

Once we sought to expand our weapons of war; now we hold a sword so powerful we dare not draw it from its scabbard.

But these changes are only the beginning. More are ahead, far more basic. They are changes in the world order—in the relationship of the United States to the world—and, in the last analysis, in our own society and our own selves.

The most obvious change, the greatest immediate threat, and the greatest need for further change, is in our concepts and methods of war. The United States is not a warlike nation; still, armed combat has always been our last resort, our last line of defense of our interests—and every generation of Americans has met its own test, made its sacrifice in battle. But now science has made war a threat to the very existence of man on this earth.

Already five nations possess the nuclear weapon, the weapon of ultimate destruction. A dozen nations now have the capacity to build nuclear arms; the cost of developing them is now well within the resources of many private business corporations. The danger is great that other nations will produce these awesome weapons —and that, once produced . . . they will be used. And once nuclear war were to start, even between small, remote countries, it would be extremely difficult, perhaps impossible, to prevent a step-by-step progression of local war into general conflagration.

Eighty million Americans—and hundreds of millions of other people—would die within the first 24 hours of a full-scale nuclear exchange. And, as Chairman Khrushchev once said, the survivors would envy the dead.

This is simply not an acceptable future—an acceptable world for our children. We must remove that sword of Damocles from the heads of the peoples of the world—from ourselves, our own families, our own children. The place to begin is by reaching an agreement which will at once prevent the further spread of nuclear weapons to any countries that do not now possess them, and then to control and eventually eliminate the weapons now in possession of the present nuclear powers.

And, as President Johnson has said, the time is now.

Columbus, Ohio
October 8, 1966

Preventing the spread of these awesome weapons has . . . become a first priority of our policy. It is clear that nothing is more important to our future.

But it is also clear that we cannot preach restraint to the rest of the world without restraining our own reliance on nuclear weapons; we cannot expect other nations to forego the same club which we ourselves are unwilling to lay down.

We must therefore pledge to the world that we will *not* be the first to use nuclear weapons against a nation which itself does not possess them. Communist China has made this pledge; and the Soviet Union . . . offered to make it if the United States would do the same.

Such a pledge would not weaken the ultimate security of the United States. It would not affect our military balance with either the Soviet Union or Red China, both of which have nuclear weapons.

It would limit our future action toward other nations: They would no longer have to fear our strategic nuclear arsenal.

And it will not be as easy to have our way if the threat of ultimate destruction is removed.

But this is a choice we must make. We must be prepared to give up some momentary military advantages to maintain our security over the long run. And, again, what is needed is determination and courage and candor.

> New York State Society of Newspaper Editors
> Utica, New York
> February 7, 1966

Communism

The greatest success for nations, as for individuals, is found in truth to themselves. We did not build the

United States on anticommunism. The strength of our institutions, the energy and talent of Americans, come out of our long struggle to build a nation of justice and freedom and happiness. Ours is the strength of positive faith; we need neither to hate nor fear our adversaries. Let our emphasis be, then, less on what the Communists are doing to threaten peace and order in Latin America—and more on what we can do to help build a better life for its people.

> "The Alliance for Progress: Symbol and Substance"
> Speech in the Senate of the United States
> May 9 and 10, 1966

I believe that if we enter the battle for the minds of tomorrow's leaders with all the vigor and dedication at our command, we will win hands down. I believe this because we have so much going for us—despite what success the articulate, highly disciplined Communist cadres have had.

First, we have the truth on our side. We can admit that everything is not perfect within our borders.

Second, we have this goodwill and respect that has largely been untapped, and the sharing of the common aspiration of peoples to be free and to be the masters of their own destinies.

Third, we have the evidence—as stark as the wall in Berlin—that wherever free societies have competed directly with Communist societies, it is freedom that has provided the greatest amount of social progress and social justice and has been the most effective in destroying ignorance, disease, hunger, and want.

> Remarks Before the Business Council
> Mayflower Hotel
> Washington, D.C.
> March 14, 1962

Ultimately, Communism must be defeated by progressive political programs which wipe out the poverty, misery, and discontent on which it thrives. For that reason, progressive political programs are the best way to erode the Communist presence in Latin America, to turn back the Communist thrust into Southeast Asia, and to insure the stability of the new African nations, and preserve stability in the world.

But however wise our efforts may be in unconventional diplomacy and unconventional warfare, however sensible our diversity of weapons and strategy, however great our military power and determined our counteroffensive of ideas, there is yet another obstacle to our opening to the future. That is the image of the future we project by our own example—what substance we provide for the international hopes we can kindle.

Thus we end where we begin. We must get our own house in order. We must because it is right. We must because it is might.

"Counterinsurgency"
The Pursuit of Justice

We live in a free and open society; that is where our strength and greatness lies. We do not hide our faults behind a wall; we do not try to bury our mistakes; we do not conceal incidents, even though they are shameful. We have no secrets from ourselves or from others. If there is an outbreak of violence in some sections of the United States, it is flashed around the world in less than an hour and quickly finds its way into the Communist propaganda mill.

And while we recognize our own faults and acknowledge our responsibilities to continue to do better, let us also recognize how much better we have done than the system with which we presently are struggling for men's souls and hearts. . . .

Yes, we have our problems in Alabama, but to be blunt, we are not shooting old women and young children in the back as the Communists are doing in Berlin. As the newspapers and people of the world freely discuss the errors of a small minority in this country and hold the entire United States responsible, the Communist officials themselves build a wall in Berlin to keep truth and freedom out—and tyranny in. Those who attempt to flee the Worker's Paradise receive a bullet—not a passport.

Can anybody equate the disturbance in Alabama last spring with the death by starvation of hundreds and hundreds of thousands of Chinese peasants under a farm-commune system which has failed?

Consider how many thousands of words have been printed around the world about Birmingham and Montgomery compared to what has been said about this systematic extinction of large numbers of Chinese by their fellow countrymen. How much more has been written about Little Rock than Tibet or even Hungary!

This is a free society. Our faults are discussed. Our mistakes make a rich grist for the Communist propaganda machine. This we accept. However, let us all remember also that their failures are seldom even mentioned, their mistakes never fully known, and the terror of their system discussed only when it becomes politically expedient. Five years after Khrushchev dies—who will be moving his body?

> National Conference of Christians and Jews
> Dinner
> Cleveland, Ohio
> December 3, 1961

The postwar revival of democratic Europe has exerted a magnetic attraction on Communist Europe. On the dark side of the iron curtain, despite rigid Communist controls, democratic ideas, democratic techniques, democratic fashions, and democratic ideals are stirring. Among its own intellectuals and its own youth, Communism finds itself on the defensive. The flow of influence is now always from West to East, not from East to West; from democracy to Communism, not from Communism to democracy.

Because the flow of influence goes one way, the flow of people goes the other. This surely is the meaning of the Berlin Wall, that ugly mass of concrete, brick, and barbed wire which lies across the heart of the city like a medieval instrument of torture. For the people of Berlin, the erection of that wall was of course an affront and a source of anguish. But I judge from peoples around the world, from my travels throughout the world, that the Berlin Wall is regarded everywhere as a proof of Communist bankruptcy, a symbol of Communist failure.

"Berlin East and West—A Controlled Experiment"
The Pursuit of Justice

There are indications today, that, while the free states are working ever more closely together, the Communist system is beginning to exhibit signs of discord and fragmentation.

Moscow says one thing, Peking another, and the still, small voice of Tirana compounds the clamor.

This discord is the inevitable result of the attempt to impose a single policy on a world dominated by national traditions and national interests. It confirms our own view that the world is moving, not toward a single centralized order, but toward a unity in diversity, with many nations developing according to their own traditions and abilities. They remain bound by respect for the rights of others, loyalty to the world community, and unshakable faith in the dignity and freedom of man.

> "The New Frontier and the New Europe"
> Beethoven Hall
> Bonn, Germany
> February 24, 1962

An analysis of the worldwide impression that our system is unpopular can reveal the source of our difficulties, our problems, and some possible solutions. First, we must recognize that in many countries . . . there is a strong and vocal Communist opposition to the United States and to our way of life. This opposition is well organized. Highly disciplined cadres concentrate their activities in universities, labor organizations, and intellectual groups. Most frequently the leaders are energetic, courageous, and articulate. They have a party line they follow rigidly. They know exactly what they think. They know where they are going, and they are willing to use any means to achieve their ends.

Within each of their countries, these groups exploit, frequently with devastating effect, the areas of differences between their country and the United States. In those countries which were formerly colonial possessions, the local inhabitants are apt to have an anti-European bias, and the Communists are frequently successful in their efforts to associate us with that antagonism. Beyond that, they take advantage of their nation's policy differences with the United States. . . .

Added to all this is the Communists' dedication. I think back to the young man who stood ten feet from me at the University of Indonesia in Djakarta and hit me across the face with a piece of hard fruit. He was willing to risk prison to demonstrate his hatred for a representative of the United States.

Against this, as I saw repeatedly, there is no one to question the Communist positions, their facts. There is no "pro-democracy" organization. There is no disciplined and calculated effort to present another side.

And so it is that a small, able and well-trained unit can take over a meeting or an organization or even a government.

> *Saturday Evening Post*
> August 25, 1962

We cannot permit a well-disciplined articulate, vocal minority to intimidate or discourage us. If we stand up and demonstrate that we are prepared to meet them face to face, that we will not be intimidated; that we will talk with them; that we will exchange views with them; that we will debate with them; yes—even that we know some students who believe in freedom of speech who if they wish it will fight them—we shall be successful; not immediately perhaps, but given the wisdom of our other policies, slowly and inexorably.

> "The Alliance for Progress: Symbol and Substance"
> Speech in the Senate of the United States
> May 9 and 10, 1966

I think that the Communist party as a political organization is of no danger to the United States. It has no following and has been disregarded by the

American people for many, many years. It has been studied; attention has been given to it by newspapers, by Congressional committees. And so everybody in the United States has had the opportunity to analyze it. The result is that it is down to a bare minimal following.

. . . An organization even as small as the Communist party is in the United States (about ten thousand members) is dominated, financed, and controlled by a foreign power. In that respect it poses a danger at all times, because it takes instructions and orders from an outside government. The danger exists not in its numbers, not in its political power in the United States, but in the fact, as the Supreme Court has held eight to one, that it is dominated, financed, and controlled by the Soviet Union.

Any time that you have a group or an organization in a country that exists for and takes instructions from an outside and hostile power, that poses a danger.

"Extremism, Left and Right"
The Pursuit of Justice

Foreign Aid

I believe that we are ready to recognize that foreign aid is not a "giveaway"—rather that it is both a moral obligation to fellow human beings and a sound and necessary investment in the future. We are incomparably richer than any other nation, now or in the history of mankind; our wealth is as great as that of all the rest of the noncommunist world put together. I believe we are ready to use this wealth for the benefit of all men. And I believe we are ready to recognize that millions saved now can mean billions lost 5 or 10 or 20 years from now and that the human cost of delay is incalculable. Time after time, in these uncertain and dangerous years, we have reaped the consequences of neglect and delay, of misery and disease, and hunger left too long to fester unremedied—in Cuba, in the Dominican Republic, in Vietnam. As President Kennedy said:

If we cannot help the many who are poor, we cannot save the few who are rich.

"The Alliance for Progress: Symbol and Substance"
Speech in the Senate of the United States
May 9 and 10, 1966

It is not given to us to right every wrong, to make perfect all the imperfections of the world. But neither is it given to us to sit content in our storehouses—dieting while others starve, buying 8 million new cars a year while most of the world goes without shoes. We are simply not doing enough.

Statement
Senate Floor
July 21, 1966

[Foreign aid] is an obligation we cannot avoid. The issue is relatively simple—do we do the job or don't we?

To many persons . . . the foreign aid program may seem remote—that the arguments for its necessity may seem abstract and intellectual rather than immediate and personal.

But surely the challenge which confronts us requires us to convert such issues from abstract necessities into personal concerns.

Many communities in this country now have in their midst students, scholars, engineers, and businessmen from foreign lands. And some communities have set up committees to make it possible for our guests to meet Americans, to learn what we are really like. But I doubt whether we have done nearly as much in this area as we should be doing. . . .

Our communities can do even more. Why should we not, for example, raise money locally each year to send some of our brightest boys and girls to schools overseas—and receive in exchange children from foreign countries in our schools? And I would add that I would not necessarily limit the exchange to countries on our side of the iron curtain. This program should not have to be done by the Federal Government or under its direction. Responsive citizens . . . could begin and put into effect such a program.

In the last analysis every issue comes at last to a set of intellectual and moral decisions within the mind and heart of each one of us as individuals. My experience every day . . . reinforces my conviction that our democracy will stand or fall on the capacity of each individual in the nation to meet his responsibilities.

Most of our fellow citizens do their best—and do it in the modest, unspectacular, decent, natural way which is the highest form of public service.

> Joint Defense Appeal of the American Jewish
> Committee and the Anti-Defamation League of
> B'nai B'rith
> Chicago, Illinois
> June 21, 1961

There is a temptation—one to which we have sometimes given in—to use our great power and our aid to force agreement from other nations or to punish them for their disagreement. This temptation is most obvious in matters of foreign policy and the Cold War: whether a country voted in the O.A.S. to approve our action in the Dominican Republic, or perhaps whether it recognizes Communist China or votes for its admission to the United Nations. These are matters of considerable importance to the United States. It is understandable that officials in the Executive branch or members of Congress or others in the country would feel that nations which fail to stand with us are not reliable allies and should not receive U.S. assistance.

But this feeling, so understandable in the passions and excitement of the moment, can only be harmful over the long run. We expect our Government to reflect the feelings of our people. Latin-Americans expect the same from their governments and deeply resent any government which seems less than fully independent in its decisions. One Latin-American President put it to me succintly: "If you want a government that says always 'yes, yes, yes,'" he told me, "you will soon have to deal with a government that says always, 'no, no, no'."

> "The Alliance for Progress: Symbol and Substance"
> Speech in the Senate of the United States
> May 9 and 10, 1966

Above all else we must be associated, in every way, through a broad array of attitudes and policies which should infuse the acts and decisions of the U.S. Government and every individual U.S. official with the goals of human dignity, social justice, and political democracy toward which economic and material progress is only a means.

No matter what we do in the economic field, if we concentrate only in the economic field, if we concentrate only on economic progress, there will be no lasting benefit, and it will not work. We must have social progress and social reforms; the people of the United States must be identified with the aspirations of the people. . . .

> "The Alliance for Progress: Symbol and Substance"
> Speech in the Senate of the United States
> May 9 and 10, 1966

Vietnam

We have to remind ourselves that the war is not over. The bombs are still falling 200 miles north of the demilitarized zone and reservists are still being called up.

Stopping the bombing must be part of a coordinated plan. The first thing we must recognize is that we will have to negotiate with the National Liberation Front. It is silly for our Government to act as if the N.L.F. does not exist. They are not going to come in just to surrender and be given their swords as we did at Appomattox and be given back their horses and told to go home for the spring plowing.

> Philadelphia
> April 2, 1968

When a hundred student body presidents and editors of college newspapers; hundreds of former Peace Corps volunteers; dozens of present Rhodes Scholars question the basic premises of the [Vietnam] war, they should not and cannot be ignored.

These students oppose the war for the brutality and the horror of all wars, and for the particular terror of this one. But for our young people, I suspect, Vietnam is a shock as it cannot be to us. They did not know World War II, or even Korea. And this is a war surrounded by rhetoric they do not understand or accept; these are the children not of the Cold War, but of the Thaw. Their memories of Communism are not of Stalin's purges and death camps, not even the terrible revelations of the Twentieth Party Congress or the streets of Hungary. They see the world as one in which Communist states can be each others' deadliest enemies or even friends of the West, in which Communism is certainly no better, but perhaps no worse, than many other evil and repressive dictatorships all around the world—with which we conclude alliances when that is felt to be in our interest.

> Remarks made at Americans for Democratic Action Dinner
> Philadelphia, Pennsylvania
> February 24, 1967

However the war may seem to us, [youth] see it as one in which the largest and most powerful nation on earth is killing children (they do not care if accidentally) in a remote and insignificant land. We speak of past commitments, of the burden of past mistakes made before many of them were born—before almost any could vote. They see us spend billions on armaments while poverty and ignorance continue at home; they see us willing to fight a war for freedom in Vietnam, but unwilling to fight with one one-hundredth the money or force or effort to secure freedom in Mississippi or Alabama or the ghettos of the North. And they see, perhaps most disturbing of all, that they are remote from the decisions of policy; that they themselves frequently do not, by the nature of our political system, share in the power of choice on great questions shaping their lives.

> Americans for Democratic Action Dinner
> Philadelphia, Pennsylvania
> February 24, 1967

We stand at the doorway of great decisions and fateful action. To decide in ignorance is to risk disaster. But if we now can clearly define our ends in South Vietnam; if we can at least begin discussing what our future relations with mainland China are to be; if we can adapt our means to those ends, and, most important, if we can use only that force—and no more—that is needed to accomplish these objectives; then there is hope that they may be achieved without prohibitive cost to ourselves, to the people of Vietnam, or to the peace of the world.

And if this debate can reach such a definition, we will know at least that we have followed the path of reason and realism as far as it now can lead.

And we will have worked to meet our responsibilities to our posterity—to walk the final mile toward peace, not so much for ourselves, as for those who will come after.

> *U.S. News & World Report*
> March 7, 1966

. . . Our military effort will mean nothing if it is not followed by a successful pacification effort which inspires the people of South Vietnam.

But we have not yet made the effort necessary.

We are spending far more on military efforts than on all the education, land reform, and welfare programs which might convince a young South Vietnamese that his future is not best served by the Communists.

And the best talent and brains in our government are focused far more on military action than they are on programs which might help the people of South Vietnam and—in the long run—help our effort as well.

This imbalance must change.

For, if we regard bombing as the answer in Vietnam, we are headed straight for disaster. In the past, bombing has not proved a decisive weapon against a rural economy—or against a guerrilla army.

And the temptation will now be to argue that if limited bombing does not produce a solution, that further bombing, more extended military action, is the answer. The danger is that the decision to resume may become the first in a series of steps on a road from which there is no turning back—a road which leads to catastrophe for all mankind. That cannot be permitted to happen.

> Statement
> Senate Floor
> January 31, 1966

We must realize that a peaceful settlement will require that both sides make some concessions—that both sides concede matters that are important in order to preserve interests which are essential.

Before we can hope to reach a settlement, therefore, our position with regard to all the critical issues must be clear at least in our own minds. That position must flow from a clear understanding of our role in Southeast Asia and in the world—and a precise assessment of the likely outcome of every course of action. For we have a responsibility—to the rest of the world and to our own children—to exert our best efforts of thought and talent and energy to find a solution—not an easy solution, for that does not exist; not a quick solution, for that does not exist—but a solution which will preserve our national interests without an even wider war in Asia.

> Democratic State Convention
> Manchester, New Hampshire
> September 23, 1966

If negotiation is our aim, as we have so clearly said it is, we must seek a middle ground. A negotiated settlement means that each side must concede matters that are important in order to preserve positions that are essential.

It may be that negotiation is not possible in this war because our political aims are irreconcilable; because one side, or both sides, are not willing to accept anything less than the fruits of victory. If that is so, then we must reluctantly let slip the hope of reasoned discussion and proceed to the uncertain, uncharted course of war.

I believe there is a middle way, that an end to the fighting and a peaceful settlement can be achieved. It must be said, before all else, that the middle way—the way of negotiation—involves risks. An adversary who lives may perhaps fight another day. And a government which is not continuously sheltered by American military power may be again attacked or subverted or overthrown.

These risks, I believe, we are courageous enough to

undertake. They are risks, in fact, which we do take every day in a hundred countries in every corner of every continent. There are dozens of countries which might be the target of Communist aggression or subversion. If we are unwilling to take any risk that they might be subverted or conquered by the Communists, we might simply have occupied all of them. But, clearly, we would rather live with such risks than attempt to occupy these nations. We take these risks because we believe men and nations will not willingly choose to submit to other men from other lands.

U.S. News & World Report
March 7, 1966

Latín America

We must understand that the people of Latin America are like the people of the United States. What they want, what they demand, are dignity and justice for themselves and for their families.

Mere economic aid is not enough. We shall not be able to buy the people of Latin America any more than we are able to buy the people of any other part of the world. We may be able to buy a few of the people, just as we are able to buy a few of the people in the United States, but the people of Latin America have the same kind of spirit, hope, trust, and desires for the future that the people here in the United States have. That fact must be recognized as we develop any . . . programs and policies, if we expect success.

> "The Alliance for Progress: Symbol and Substance"
> Speech in the Senate of the United States
> May 9 and 10, 1966

. . . There is one element of our policy that must be clear—one constant thread running through all our days:

That we associate ourselves with the aspirations of the Latin-American people for a better life—for justice between men and nations—for the dignity of freedom and self-sufficiency. These demands are in part material; above all, they are demands of the spirit.

But we must realize that the demands of the spirit— the demands for justice and a sense of participation in the life of one's country—are the essential precondition to material progress. The dispossessed and the landless will not strive and sacrifice to improve land they do not share. Parents will not sacrifice to insure education for their children, the children themselves will not study, if the schools to which they go end in the third grade, and if they are considered unfit for admission to higher grades. Individual entrepeneurs will not flourish in a closed society, a society which reserves all wealth and power and privilege for the same classes, the same families, which have held that wealth and power for the last 300 years.

We will understand the demands of justice—and help to meet them—only by a renewed consciousness and dedication to our own heritage, to the dreams of liberty and justice which have sustained this nation since our birth in revolution less than two centuries ago.

> "The Alliance for Progress: Symbol and Substance"
> Speech in the Senate of the United States
> May 9 and 10, 1966

This we must clearly understand: Communism is not a native growth in Latin America. Given any meaningful alternative, its people will reject Communism and follow the path of democratic reform and membership in the interamerican system. But if we allow ourselves to become allied with those to whom the cry of "Communism!" is only an excuse for the perpetuation of privilege—if we assist, with military material and other aid, governments which use that aid to prevent reform for their people—then we will give the Communists a strength which they can not attain by anything they themselves might do.

President Johnson's Mexico City Address set what must be our policy: "We will not be deterred," he said, "by those who say that to risk change is to risk Communism."

> "The Alliance for Progress: Symbol and Substance"
> Speech in the Senate of the United States
> May 9 and 10, 1966

Education is the second major problem embracing both progress and justice. And it is of primary importance to Latin America—as to every nation.

Education is not only important to understanding the world and each other—it is the key to the future, the foundation of progress in the modern world. No nation, not one, has entered the ranks of modern economic society without trained and educated people to run the factories, manage institutions, guide the government, draw plans. Without them, all the money and loans are worthless.

Education is the key to progress of another kind: like land reform, it is a passport to citizenship. As Horace Mann put it:

A human being is not, in any proper sense, a human being until he is educated.

Men without education are condemned to lives as outsiders—outside political life, outside the twentieth century, foreigners in their own land. Men who are illiterate cannot read newspapers or instruction manuals or even the road signs by which we guide our footsteps. Even for those who can read, further education is the key to social and economic mobility and freedom; there can be no career open to the talents without the education which develops talent.

> "The Alliance for Progress: Symbol and Substance"
> Speech in the Senate of the United States
> May 9 and 10, 1966

Four

THE WIT OF ROBERT F. KENNEDY

In 1904 Senator Robert Kennedy, then the ... of maps, received a letter from a seven-year-old boy upstate Long Island boy who asked, "Do you ...

In 1966 Senator Robert Kennedy, then the father of nine, received a letter from a seven-year-old Farmingdale, Long Island boy who asked, "Do you take good care of your children?"

The Senator decided that the issue was worth sharing with the rest of his constituents, so in his September newsletter he quoted the little boy's query and replied: "I asked my children and they voted 'yes' by 4 to 3 with 2 abstentions."

At a recent public affair, when motion picture producer Dore Schary introduced him in particularly glowing terms, Bobby rose and dryly observed, "I've been called a lot of things in my life, but this is the first time I've been called 'beloved.'"

Senator Robert F. Kennedy delivered this little piece of self-mockery at the Women's National Press Club dinner for the new Congress in 1965: "I want to assure you I have no Presidential aspirations—nor does my wife, Ethel Bird."

Once Bobby Kennedy's young daughter Kerry rushed up to him, threw her arms around him, and gave him a loving kiss on the cheek. Said Bobby, teasingly, "Please Kerry, I told you—only when there are cameramen around."

RFK once spoke with an author who was writing a book about him, and asked the writer how he looked in the book. Replied the writer, "Like a million dollars." Quipped Bobby, "That's awfully low for a Kennedy."

During the Senate Foreign Relations Committee hearings early in 1966, Senator Robert Kennedy became increasingly concerned that the issue of what role—if any—the Viet Cong would play in Vietnamese peace talks was being avoided. He put his staff of speech writers to work on a statement of his position on that issue, and delivered his unsolicited minority opinion at a well-covered press conference the next day. When one reporter asked him what he planned to do next with his proposals, Kennedy smiled and shrugged, "I guess I'll take them home and show them to my wife."

In 1965 Senator Robert Kennedy addressed the International Radio and TV Society on the subject of foreign aid, advocating assistance in "programs of family planning" for foreign nations who requested it. Suddenly Kennedy stopped, turned to his wife, and said "You'd better leave."

In 1966, almost two full years after he had been elected as Senator from New York, Robert Kennedy received in the mail a form letter from Democratic National Chairman John Bailey. The letter had been forwarded from Kennedy's former voting address,

Barnstable, Mass. The Senator mailed the letter back to Bailey with this note added:

"Dear John—I moved. Bob."

Accused of "carpetbagging" in his bid for New York's Senatorial seat, Robert Kennedy nevertheless won the election and jokingly twitted himself about it at the 1965 Women's National Press Club Dinner: "I can't tell you how happy I am to be here representing the great state of . . . ah . . . ah . . . ."

At the time when Senator Robert Kennedy announced his proposal that the Viet Cong comprise a part of the peacetime government of Vietnam, Vice President Humphrey was visiting that embattled country. As the controversial proposals made news, Humphrey commented that Kennedy's idea "was like putting a fox in the chicken coop."

When the Vice President returned to Washington he found this letter from Bobby on his desk:

Dear Hubert,
Welcome home. I was taking care of everything back here while you were away. Perhaps you heard. As a matter of fact, I felt a little like a fox in the chicken house myself.
Congratulations on your trip.
Best, Bob.

As a Senator from New York, Robert Kennedy once observed that there seemed to be a close alliance between the stage and politics in that state. He speculated in 1965 that many New York politicos might be quite at home on Broadway.

"For instance," suggested the Senator, "John Lindsay starring in *All in Good Time;* Adam Clayton Powell as the lead in *Catch Me if You Can;* Mayor Wagner and Governor Rockefeller in *The Odd Couple* or *Two for the Seesaw;* Senator Javits in *Fade Out-Fade In;* and Winthrop Aldrich is being groomed for the lead in *The Man From UNCLE*.

"Finally," concluded Bobby, "they're writing a new version of *Luv,* costarring President Johnson and me."

Robert Kennedy is well aware of the fact that Vice President Hubert Humphrey is constantly bombarded with assertions that the New York Senator is his foremost rival for the 1972 Presidential nomination. One of Bobby's more rabid boosters wrote him a letter in which, certain that Kennedy was sure to be President one day, he asked for an advance copy of his Inaugural Address. Seizing the opportunity to rib the Vice President, Bobby sent the letter to Humphrey along with this note: "Dear Mr. Vice President. I thought you would like to see a typical sample of my mail . . . Bob."

Robert Kennedy's address at the 1965 edition of the Baseball Writers' dinner:

"I can't believe all those things Ted Williams says about you fellows is true.

"Since my election, I've received many invitations for speaking engagements—from the Overseas Press Club to the Puerto Rican forum. It seems they want me to speak everywhere but on the floor of the Senate.

"I am delighted to see Johnny Keane here tonight—he's new to New York—I'm his guide.

"One of the writers here said that last November I stole home and it wasn't even my home. Being originally from Massachusetts, I was automatically a Yankee. But during the last campaign, I kept hearing 'Yankee go home.'

"I'm also glad to see Yogi Berra here. I understand he is writing a book: *Lucky to be a Yankee*. By Yogi Berra, as told to Mel Allen.

"I've also been talking to Joe Cronin. I remember in 1961, when Dave Powers, who is a great baseball fan, brought Joe Cronin into President Kennedy's office to present the traditional baseball pass. President Kennedy said, 'Dave, what was that story you told me about Joe Cronin?'

"Dave looked at Cronin and said, 'Lifetime average of .302?'

"The President said, 'No.'

" 'Hall of Fame?'

"The President said, 'No.'

" 'Mr. President, you must mean the time Carl Hubbell struck out five Hall of Famers in a row—Ruth, Gehrig, Foxx, Simmons, and Joe Cronin.'

" 'Yes, that's the story.'

"And Joe said, 'Mr. President, it's a pleasure to strike out in such company.'

"I enjoy baseball and I found last year's pennant races very exciting. In the National League they couldn't decide who the leader was until the very last day. It sounds like the New York Legislature.

"A number of people here have asked me about that situation. I want to make it clear that there is no truth to reports that I am manager of the Albany Democrats.

"What they're doing up there reminds me of the time when Wilbert Robinson was managing the Brooklyn Dodgers, and three of them arrived at third base at the same time. They asked Uncle Robbie whether he was upset. He said, 'Hell, no, that's the closest those fellows have been to each other all season.'

"I have nine children now—enough for a baseball team. We'll be training soon. Maybe Frank Lane will buy us.

"With all these children I've decided to run my house like the Senate. We have a new speaker. We're working on a Medicare program. But the rest of the family doesn't seem to want to follow the seniority rule.

"The other day a bell rang and I got ready to go to vote. But Ethel said it was just the signal for the four o'clock feeding. . . .

"Speaking seriously, baseball has been our national sport for almost a hundred years. Other sports may be faster, or more exciting on television, but baseball is much more than a spectator sport. When you go out on a nice day, in every playground and vacant lot you will find them playing baseball. It is a part of every man's life. It is a part of our country and will continue to be. As Grantland Rice once said, 'From one old cat to the last at bat.'

"Some say that baseball is on the way down. But as long as young boys have heroes, and as long as the players and owners and all of you meet your responsibilities, I think baseball is on the way up.

"Finally, let me say that I did not run for the Senate to become Commissioner of Baseball. I'm not interested in the position because it doesn't have enough power."

In August, 1965 Senator Robert Kennedy was concluding some remarks honoring forty-three graduates of a VISTA training program. One of the trainees suggested that Kennedy officially swear them in, whereupon Kennedy, finding out that there was no official oath, made up his own: "Repeat after me. I swear that I will be a good VISTA volunteer. I will assist those in need, help my U.S. Senator all I can, and otherwise behave myself. So help me God."

Returning from a 1966 trip to South Africa, Robert F. Kennedy, always the focus of much controversy, was not surprised to find himself the target of some criticism. At the inevitable impromptu news conference, a reporter mentioned that Senator Wayne Morse had asserted that he would support Kennedy if he ran for the Presidency in 1968. Kennedy denied any interest in public office other than his Senate seat, and added dryly, "But I'm grateful for any kind words that were said about me by anyone while I was gone."

On October 22, 1966, Senator Robert Kennedy traveled to the University of California's Berkeley Campus to address the school's students, whose political militancy had been making worldwide newspaper headlines for some time. Referring to Bishop George Berkeley, for whom the city was named, Kennedy said:

". . . The man who said 'ferments of the worst kind succeed to perfect inaction,' also advised us that 'our youth we can have today. We may always find time to grow old.' And even if all of you do not heed the first maxim, you seem to be busily following the second —or at least that's what my advisers tell me it says in the magazines.

"After all, you are the first college to become a major political issue since George III attacked Harvard for being a center of rebellion and subversion. And he was right."

In 1965 Robert Kennedy thought back to the exciting moments before he began his final assault of the last and steepest ridge separating him from the peak of Mt. Kennedy:

"I remembered my mother's last words to me: 'Don't slip, dear,' and the admonition of a friend who had obviously never climbed: 'Don't look down.' And I remembered what my son, Joe, said on the telephone as I was about to leave Seattle: 'Good luck, Daddy. You'll need it.' And the reporter from a national newspaper covering the climb told me before I began that his paper had just completed my obituary."

On January 12, 1967, Senator Robert Kennedy addressed the Democratic delegates to New York State's Constitutional Convention in Albany. After referring to the nearly miraculous work of the Constitutional Convention at Philadelphia in 1787, Kennedy went on to ask:

"Can we have a miracle at Albany? Perhaps our commitment to separation of church and state prevents that kind of goal—but I will tell you—for the kind of money New York is spending, we have a right to ask each of the delegates to seek some providential guidance...."

Speaking before the 1966 luncheon for the Federation of Jewish Philanthropies, Senator Robert Kennedy found himself following the famous lawyer and eloquent speaker, Louis Nizer. Kennedy used this analogy to convey his feelings about such a situation: "A man bored everyone he met by relating his experiences during the Johnstown flood.... When he died, he asked

Saint Peter to gather an audience so that he could tell them his story of the Johnstown flood. Saint Peter agreed, but warned him: 'Remember, Noah will be in the audience.' "

Early in 1966, Senator Robert F. Kennedy spoke at the University of Mississippi, where he was reminded of the incidents precipitated by the admission of James Meredith, a Negro, to the university several years earlier. The Senator recalled some of the action that took place behind the scenes prior to the disturbances. Kennedy, then Attorney General, had had about twenty-five telephone talks with Governor Ross Barnett, who wanted him to send federal marshals to the school with orders to draw their guns if challenged. Ross knew that it would then seem to Mississippians that he was backing down to the Federal Government only when confronted with superior force.

Recounted Kennedy, "I said I would have the Chief Marshal pull his gun. He called back in a little while and said he had talked with his advisers in Jackson, and *all* the marshals would have to pull their guns."

Seeing that President Johnson's "Great Society" concept had become a byword on the nation's lips, New York State's Governor Nelson Rockefeller decided to adopt the "Just Society" as a catchy slogan for his 1966 reelection campaign. Taking due note of this phenomenon in an address before a Democratic meeting in Albany, Senator Robert Kennedy took the trend to its logical conclusion: "What we really need, gentlemen," deadpanned Bobby, "is a *Just Great* Society."

Organizing the entire Robert F. Kennedy family for an outing of any kind is a formidable problem in logistics. On one occasion Bobby lined up his nine children and told them, "We're all going to a convention—now be good. I have something for the one who's best."

The brood turned to file out, when their father added, "And one more thing—I'll *also* have something for the one who's worst."

On one occasion Robert F. Kennedy was inspecting the Hudson River, notorious for its high level of pollution around New York City. Taking one sniff of a beaker of the fetid river water, Kennedy wrinkled up his nose and cracked, "If you fall into this river, you won't drown—you'll decay!"

During the 1965 Mayoralty elections in New York City, Robert Kennedy was asked to campaign for Democratic candidate Abe Beam, who was losing some of the formerly Democratic neighborhoods in the city. In one such predominantly Irish neighborhood, Bobby exhorted the adults to return to the party of their fathers: "Don't you know we are all Democrats? We are the party of Roosevelt, Truman, Kennedy, Johnson, and . . . " Kennedy paused for a moment, scanning the multitude of Irish faces in the audience, and, smiling, concluded, " . . . Huey Long!"

The extensive Kennedy family campaigns as a unit when any of its members are involved in a political contest. Robert Kennedy, as well as his mother, wife, brother and sisters, campaigned vigorously for his brother John in all of his political races, and is credited with this concise speech at one rally during John's 1952 Senatorial campaign against Henry Cabot Lodge:

"My brother Jack couldn't be here. My mother couldn't be here. My sister Eunice couldn't be here, my sister Pat couldn't be here, my sister Jean couldn't be here, but if my brother Jack were here he'd tell you Lodge has a very bad voting record."

In some of his addresses as Attorney General, Robert Kennedy enjoyed telling this anecdote about the time he was talking to a certain businessman:

"I don't trust your brother," the businessman scolded.

"My brother, the President?" asked Kennedy.

"No, your brother, Ted," was the reply. "And furthermore, you're listening too much to Arthur."

"Arthur Schlesinger?" suggested Bobby.

"No, Arthur Goldberg," answered the businessman. "What's more, you should take more advice from Rose."

"Alex Rose, the New York Liberal Party leader?"

"No, your mother, Rose," the businessman said.

At the California Institute of Technology, in June, 1964, Robert Kennedy began a speech in a somewhat unorthodox way:

"Many of you, I know, are approaching the end of your schooling. The time of graduation—and liberation—is upon you. This is a time when you must expect to endure a good many profound remarks about your past and your future, your obligations and your challenges.

I hesitate to afflict you further—and am consoled only by the fact that I went through a comparable ordeal when I finished college a few years back and I can recall not one word of what was said. This gives me, I might add, a pleasant sense of irresponsibility today."

In the 1960 Presidential elections Teamster boss Jimmy Hoffa enlisted the support of his and several other unions against John F. Kennedy. Managing J.F.K.'s campaign was Robert F. Kennedy, who even then was an enemy of Hoffa, and who, as Attorney General, would eventually help put the union leader behind bars. Yet, when Joey Gallo, a notorious Brooklyn gangster, offered to use his power to help Bobby campaign for Jack, Bobby told him, "Just tell everybody you're voting for Nixon."

Robert Kennedy told about one memorable visit on his trip to Rome:

"We had a friendly audience with Pope John. . . . He blessed us all, including the American newspapermen who were traveling with us, most of whom were not Catholics. He assured them that it was just a little blessing and wouldn't do them any harm."

On the day that John F. Kennedy was elected President in 1960, the family played a spirited game of touch football on the lawn of their Hyannis Port home. Bobby was playing quarterback, while Jack played end. On one play Jack moved downfield for a pass. In the clear for a moment, Jack reached up for the ball, but as the defense closed in on him he dropped it. Quipped the quarterback, Bobby, "That's my brother. All guts, no brains."

In January, 1963, one newsman asked Robert Kennedy if having a brother who was President were not a problem for him at times. Answered Bobby, "I don't find it so. It might be for him, but it isn't for me."

People were always concerned about the relationship of Robert Kennedy and his brother John, when J.F.K. was in the White House. Robert remarked that many people seemed to overlook the fact that the two men had been closely allied long before John became President. Stated Bobby in January, 1963: "I've been associated with the present incumbent in the White House for thirty-seven years, the first few of which were slow."

"It gives me particular pleasure to take part in this annual observance of Law Day in Virginia. I am not only a resident of Virginia, but I came here fourteen years ago as a student—and I hold Mr. Jefferson's university at Charlottesville largely responsible for any gaps or lapses in my knowledge of the law."

> Law Day Ceremonies of the
> Virginia State Bar
> Roanoke, Virginia
> May 1, 1962

John F. Kennedy was a runaway winner in his 1960 Presidential primary race in West Virginia. At a celebration following the closing of the polls, Ethel Kennedy went around snapping pictures and exclaiming, "Isn't it exciting?" Confessed the blasé Robert Kennedy to reporters, "I couldn't have done it without my brother."

Robert F. Kennedy addressing a graduating class at Marquette University: "Years ago, I was a hardworking lawyer making $4,200 a year. I took my work home every night and was very diligent. Ten years later I became the Attorney General of the United States. So, you see, if you want to become successful, just get your brother elected President."

A lawyer in the Justice Department was discussing a certain business that was allowed to deteriorate by the founder's son, when the then Attorney General Robert Kennedy remarked, "That's one mistake our father never made—taking us into business with him."

Early in 1963 Attorney General Robert Kennedy was mistakenly given a telephone call for "Senator Kennedy." Quipped Bobby, "That's how it goes. First they mistook me for Jack, and now, Teddy."

Addressing the Linn County Veterans' Council during the 1962 Veterans' Day program at Albany, Oregon, Attorney General Robert Kennedy remarked:

"Sometimes I think every resident of your state is a self-appointed missionary to convert misguided Easterners who say 'Ore—gonn.'

"Perhaps the best job ever done along this line was by L.H. Gregory, the widely known sports editor of the *Oregonian*. Some years ago, he told a Texas audience that he, too, greatly appreciated their hospitality to him, but that if they persisted in pronouncing Oregon with the accent on the last syllable, he would have to start accenting Texas in the same way."

Prior to 1960, Mrs. Arthur Schlesinger, Jr., was a staunch supporter of Adlai Stevenson, to the vexation of her husband. Confronting Mr. Schlesinger with this fact, Robert Kennedy once asked, "Can't you control your own wife, or are you like me?"

During his visit to Tokyo in 1962, Attorney General Robert Kennedy related this story: "A man asked for a judgeship for his brother. I declined—I received the inevitable phone call. He said, 'After all, your brother appointed you Attorney General.'

"I answered, 'We only serve the will of the President.'"

Attorney General Robert Kennedy addressed the commencement exercises at Manhattan College in New York City on June 12, 1962. After receiving an honorary degree the Attorney General commented:

"To receive this recognition without the normal academic niceties of attendance, absorption, and exams—not to mention tuition—does not really detract too much from the pleasure of the award. In fact, I most strongly advocate the merit system now in vogue at Manhattan College.

"I could, I know, express this simple word of thanks and subside into silence, to the accompaniment of your grateful sighs of relief. I agree that the commencement exercises at all colleges should be an elective. The long elocution lavished on captive graduates represents the final on-campus sacrifice you will be constrained to offer up for some worthy intention.

"A truly Christian Brother briefed me on the ground rules of your more recent commencements. He actually used the word 'brief.' He alluded delicately to the 1888 graduation when the visiting archbishop of San Luis Potosi, was called upon merely to give a final blessing to Cardinal Hayes' graduating class. He spoke ornately, and occasionally in English, for almost two hours.

"On these otherwise glad occasions, pundits in possession of the podium are tempted, by tradition, to reveal the accumulated wisdom of a long and mature experience. For me, this is rather easy; but as Brother A. Joseph, my mentor, discreetly hinted, even seniors seldom learn from second-hand experience—and never do on commencement day.

"Yet paradoxically, in connection with this very occasion, I, myself, have learned a lot from experience—the experience and history of your college. 159 pages . . ."

Kennedy then went on to trace the founding and growth of the Catholic institution:

"The cunning Christian Brothers, real estate experts, bought the wrong sites three times, the back of the old college became the front, new stories were added to old buildings at the bottom and the college was sold for taxes once.

"It has had at times classrooms and no students and at other times students without classrooms.

"I mention these four things not to suggest that miscalculations are not confined to Washington, to any political party or era but rather as dramatic proof of what basic unity, solidarity, loyalty, good will, and a sense of sacrifice could do against handicaps and great odds in a world beyond Manhattan."

When Robert Kennedy had finished his address to the students of Waseda University in Japan, a young cheerleader came forward to lead the students in their school song. As Bobby himself tells it, "During the first chorus he accidentally struck my wife in the pit of the stomach. She said it didn't hurt, or at least not nearly so much as it would have if he hadn't been a friend."

Robert Kennedy drew big crowds wherever he went in Poland. In Cracow the mayor asked him if he intended to run for President, to which Bobby replied, "No, I don't think I'll run for President. I think I'll run for mayor of Cracow."

At one stop on his trip to Korea, Robert Kennedy received a short briefing from a certain Army general. Later Kennedy said to a friend, "I don't want to worry you. But you remember that general who explained how we would handle the North Koreans if they attacked?

Well, the last time I saw him was two years ago in Berlin when he told us what we would do if the Russians ever moved in on us there. The only other time I saw him was when he was holding a briefing on the Bay of Pigs operation."

Speaking before the 1961 Dinner of Champions in New York City, Attorney General Robert F. Kennedy remarked:

"Standing here, surrounded by so many athletes, I feel I ought to present my credentials. I come from a family that has always emphasized and enjoyed sports —golf, tennis, football, baseball, and the rest. Last year, for instance, we did considerable running."

Robert Kennedy visited a Buddhist temple in Osaka during his trip to Japan in 1962. When a priest gave him a stick of incense to burn, Kennedy turned to Ambassador Edwin O. Reischauer and asked if such a gesture would be allowed. Reischauer informed him that it would merely be a demonstration of respect, but Kennedy, a Roman Catholic, again asked, "You're sure it won't look as if I'm worshipping Buddha?" The Ambassador reassured him that it was all right. Finally Kennedy gingerly picked up the stick of incense, and muttered under his breath, "If I get kicked out—"

Speaking before a group of foreign correspondents in Tokyo during his 1962 visit to Japan, Robert Kennedy said: "I had seaweed for breakfast yesterday. To tell you the honest-to-goodness truth, it didn't taste bad. When I went to Central Asia with Justice Douglas in 1955, they brought in a goat, very dead, plucked out its eyes, and served them to us. Justice Douglas turned to me and said, 'For the sake of America, Bob, make like it's an oyster!' So things have gone up since then."

During his official visit to Japan in 1962, relates Robert Kennedy, he spoke at Nihon University, where "... there were no heating facilities in the building but the university officials made arrangements to keep at least one part of us warm by placing electric cushions on our chairs. This can be slightly disconcerting, especially when you can't find the switch to turn it off."

In a 1962 address before the American Booksellers Association, Attorney General Robert Kennedy was advocating the sharing of our technical publications with the developing countries abroad. He mentioned that there are many good Government Printing Office publications on government and history which might be useful abroad, and then quipped:

"Incidentally, we in the government are sometimes accused of being unimaginative. I was interested to find out that one of the GPO pamphlets on the technicalities of growing tomatoes is entitled 'Hot Beds and Cold Frames.' That title should do well in any market."

The throngs that turned out for Robert Kennedy in

Poland once delayed his arrival at a dinner. The Polish Communist officials were annoyed with Kennedy's "playing to the crowds," and rebuked him. "Premier Gomulka never does," they chided.

"Well," replied the exuberant Kennedy, "maybe that's the problem."

Recalled Robert Kennedy about his visit to Japan: "It did seem embarrassing to me to come to the end of a meeting with the Foreign Minister of Japan and then suddenly thrust on him an autographed photograph of myself. I could imagine his sick smile as he opened it and said, 'Just what I always wanted . . . .' (When I gave the picture to one of the ministers, I told him that at least it was a nice frame and that he could take my picture out and replace it with one of his wife.)"

Asked in early 1963 if he cared to guess who would be the Republicans' choice of candidates in the 1964 Presidential race, Robert Kennedy answered, "Well, I know, but I don't think he does, so I don't think I'd better say."

Leaving the Overseas Press Club one evening, Robert Kennedy suddenly found himself surrounded by a group of nuns. "It's one of the great unsolved mysteries," remarked Kennedy. "All the nuns love me and none of the priests do."

Robert Kennedy is a hard-working public official, his duties occasionally claiming his time even on holidays. One Washington's Birthday during his Attorney Generalship, Kennedy noticed a few automobiles parked in the Justices' parking spots and took down their license numbers so that he could write each one of them a letter of commendation. Unexpectedly, one wrote back, "I cannot tell a lie on Washington's Birthday—I used my parking space but I went to the movies."

Replied Kennedy, "With honesty like yours, our country's cherry trees are safe."

Robert Kennedy decided to take some time off for a skiing trip in 1964. But when a visitor to his office told Kennedy that he was glad he was getting away, Bobby said, "You're the ninth person to tell me that today. What's everybody plotting here, a palace coup?"

In 1962 Robert F. Kennedy spoke at the dedication of Kendrick Hall at the University of San Francisco Law School:

". . . I am advisedly aware that you have spent two long days now celebrating your law school's golden anniversary. I suspect that the greatest virtue in any more oratory will be in its blessed brevity. If I had any doubts on this score, Father Callahan's letter of invitation delicately enlightened me. He mentioned that Father Connoly was recovering from a spinal disc operation and also that the affair did not have to last too long. I am not clear whether he was whispering a hint, a hope, or a prayer. You can never be sure with

Father Callahan. But I'll try to keep in mind that any old place in a speech is a wonderful place to stop. I would not want any speech-induced discomfort of Father Connoly to become a widespread affliction of this assemblage."

In 1962 Attorney General Robert Kennedy's office was in charge of soliciting contributions from American businessmen for the liberation of Castro's prisoners from Cuba. As Kennedy tells it, some business leaders made contributions out of humanitarian ideals, some because they knew the donations would be tax-deductible anyway, and others "perhaps felt they'd like to have a warmer relationship with the Government."

At the height of the civil rights disturbances in Oxford, Mississippi, in 1962, Attorney General Robert Kennedy received a telephone call from an aide who reported that the embattled Justice Department officers at the university campus felt like the defenders of the Alamo. "Well," Kennedy drolly reminded the aide, "you know what happened to those guys."

In 1964, as Attorney General, Robert F. Kennedy addressed the Herbert H. Lehman Human Relations Award Dinner of the American Jewish Committee Appeal for Human Relations:

"I met this afternoon with members of the American

Society of Newspaper Editors in Washington and we got along well, perhaps because some of them realized I used to be a newspaperman myself. I don't think I can lay claim to quite as close a hand at this gathering."

In 1957 Robert F. Kennedy undertook an extremely unpopular investigation in Portland, Oregon, with the result that he was not a particularly welcome figure in that city thereafter. Kennedy, for that matter, bore little love for Portland in his heart. As his plane touched down there in 1962, the Attorney General said to his companions, "Let's jump out, punch the first guy we see in the nose, jump right back into this thing, and get out of here."

Robert Kennedy was once asked his opinion of union leader Jimmy Hoffa's professed intent of organizing major league baseball players. His response: "I hope he doesn't get to first base."

Arriving late at a Business Council Meeting in Washington, Attorney General Robert Kennedy apologized and said that he owed his tardiness to "a suit filed by the Dupont Company to require the Justice Department to divest itself of the Antitrust Division."

James Bennett was the guest of honor at a Washington party celebrating his twenty-fifth year as chief of the federal prison system. He was in the process of slicing his large birthday cake when he struck a hard object. After poking around in the cake for a moment, Bennett finally came up with the obstacle, an eight-inch file, hidden there by none other than Robert F. Kennedy.

Deciding to run for the Senate seat from New York was a most difficult problem for Robert Kennedy. He was burdened with the worry of a possible defeat, as he revealed in a remark he made in August of 1964: "I don't want to become a retired elder statesman at thirty-eight."

Robert Kennedy knew that in order to win the 1964 Senatorial race he would have to rid himself of his image as a cold and calculating politician, an image he felt was inaccurate and undeserved. He was successful enough to win the election, after which one reporter asked him whether he was relieved to be done with the grueling campaign. "Yes," replied Bobby, who then smiled and quipped, "Now I can go back to being ruthless again. . . ."

Following the Democratic Nominating Convention of 1964, the Robert Kennedys were planning to hold a large and festive reception for the delegates. Every last detail of the arrangements was carefully attended to, with the exception of the mailing of the delegates' invitations. When the grievous oversight was discovered,

"Kennedy hostesses" began to invite random passersby in to fill up the party. When Bobby Kennedy finally learned of the error, he nodded his head and quipped, "I knew there was something wrong. Not enough people were wearing delegate badges, and too many were carrying boxes marked Macy's."

As soon as his 1964 Senate victory had been assured, Robert Kennedy fulfilled his campaign promise to return to his very first stop on the campaign trail. At 3:30 a.m. on the morning following his election, he traveled down to the famed Fulton Fish Market on Manhattan's Lower East Side. Remarked a relieved Kennedy, "It smells a lot better down here now."

As a newly elected Senator from New York, Robert F. Kennedy was near the bottom of the priority list for Senate seats. Remarked Bobby, "I had better seats for *Hello, Dolly!*"

On the day in January, 1965, that the newly elected Robert Kennedy was to make his Senatorial debut, his brother, Senator Edward M. Kennedy, came by in his car to pick him up. Getting behind the wheel, Bobby quipped, "Which way do I drive, Eddie? You know this routine now."

Addressing the young people in one city on his 1964 campaign tour, Robert Kennedy said, "Back in the last town, I saw a sign that read, 'Respectable Young People for Keating.' Well, I don't know where that leaves you."

A television network official was trying to smooth some ruffled feelings after an unfortunate incident at the studio during Robert F. Kennedy's 1964 campaign for the Senate. "We just try to do our best," said the official.

"That's all right," replied RFK, "we'll try to make up for your shortcomings."

Robert Kennedy commenting on the enthusiastic welcome he received in Jamestown, New York on his campaign visit: "I see my Long Island accent got you."

While he was speaking to the crowd at the airport, the roar of an airliner taking off drowned out his voice. As the noise died Kennedy pointed to the rising jet and quipped, "He's on his way back to Phoenix to report."

At one point in his campaign for the Senate seat from New York, Robert F. Kennedy observed, "I lived in New York for many years, but if this election is to be decided on the basis of who's lived here the longest, perhaps we should just elect the oldest man in the state."

Campaigning in the birthplace of his Republican opponent in the 1964 Senatorial race, Robert Kennedy used the ironic situation to twit Senator Keating: "It gives me a deep sense of satisfaction to come here to Rochester, since I know it is the home town of a distinguished white-haired American ... and I am referring, of course, to Susan B. Anthony."

By stapling new names over their old "Welcome Ted Kennedy" signs, economy-minded people in Massena, New York succeeded in creating a perfectly passable bunch of "Welcome Bob Kennedy" signs for the candidate's 1964 campaign visit to their town. When Bobby noticed this phenomenon he tore his name off one sign and, showing it to the crowd, said, "There's one big advantage to electing me. It will be cheaper for everybody. We can interchange signs with Massachusetts."

Candidate Robert Kennedy arrived several hours behind schedule for his campaign speech in Glens Falls, New York. Relieved to find the crowds still waiting for him, he expressed his gratitude for their patience, sighing, "Well, here we are five hours late. That's the well-oiled Kennedy machine for you."

There were allegations that Attorney General Robert Kennedy had decided to enter the 1964 Senatorial race at the behest of New York's "bosses." In one city, mobs of Kennedy-rooters crowded into the lobby of Kennedy's hotel, whereupon the candidate observed, "I am delighted to see so many bosses here to welcome me."

The advertising agency handling his 1964 Senatorial campaign informed Robert Kennedy that there were only three "fliers" in actual distribution, although another thirty-eight layouts were being prepared for circulation. Cracked Bobby, "Another week and you won't have to print anything. You can hand out the layouts."

When Bobby Kennedy stopped at Batavia, New York for a Senatorial campaign speech, he noticed a group of six young girls who carried a sign proclaiming that they were from a nearby town called Kennedy. Quipped Kennedy, "You see? They talk about my being a carpetbagger and I even have a city named after me."

When, in July, 1964, Robert Kennedy was asked whether he would consider entering into Massachusetts politics, he shook his head negatively and replied, impishly, "I'd be a carpetbagger there."

A woman in Saranac, New York once boarded the Kennedy family's private plane by mistake, and was taken aback to find therein Mrs. John F. Kennedy, Robert Kennedy, and a number of assorted children. "She was a very nice woman," said Robert later, "but she thought it was very crowded for a commercial plane."

At one stop on Robert Kennedy's 1964 campaign tour both he and his wife were surrounded by autograph seekers. After a while Robert was able to free himself and make his way to the waiting car, but Ethel remained behind to sign autographs. "Ethel," Bobby finally implored "*I'm* the candidate."

During the summer of 1964 a number of celebrities sponsored an outdoor campaign rally for Robert F. Kennedy. At one point in the exuberant goings-on Kennedy joined his friend Sammy Davis, Jr. for a lovely duet and cracked, "If things don't go well on November 3rd, we can go on tour."

A wildly excited crowd in Buffalo, N.Y. gave Bobby Kennedy one of the most enthusiastic receptions he got during his 1964 campaign. RFK fans cheered, screamed, pushed and fought in an attempt to get close enough to shake his hand. Later that evening the candidate attended a more decorous reception and quipped, "I've been all over the state talking Medicare today and when I came into Buffalo tonight I thought I needed it myself."

During the 1964 Senatorial campaign Robert Kennedy put in an appearance on Barry Gray's New York radio discussion show. At one point Gray pointed out that his broadcast had quite a large audience, and Kennedy responded, "I always knew you had a large audience; everywhere I go in this state there's a group of people shouting, 'We want Barry.' "

When a youngster asked Robert Kennedy why he had left Riverdale, New York as a child, Bobby told him, "I didn't want to leave. I was three years old at the time and I pleaded with my mother, 'Why must we leave Riverdale?' But we left anyway."

Republican Senator Kenneth Keating was *The New York Times*' choice in the 1964 Senate race in New York. But this factor did not trouble Robert Kennedy too much: "Well, at least they can never say I got my job through *The New York Times*."

During the summer of 1964 rumors were thick that Robert F. Kennedy would attempt to get the Democratic nomination for Vice-President. But in August President Johnson ruled out all Cabinet officers as possible candidates, a move interpreted by some as a way of deliberately eliminating Attorney General Kennedy without alienating his backers.

Shortly following Johnson's announcement Kennedy was addressing a school for Congressional candidates, and quipped, "I must confess I stand in awe of you. You are not members of the Cabinet. Therefore you are eligible for Vice-President. I've decided to send a little note to Cabinet members in general, saying, 'I'm sorry I took so many nice fellows over the side with me.'"

Senatorial candidate Robert F. Kennedy was a guest at a cocktail party attended by the political columnists for New York City's newspapers and magazines. During the evening one young woman came up to him and said, "I'm with the New York *Post,* and this is my first campaign."

"Mine too," answered Kennedy. "We'd better stay close together."

At one campaign stop in 1964 Robert Kennedy opened his speech with these remarks: "A few months ago while I was having breakfast with my wife, I was reading in the papers that California had replaced New York as the number-one state in population—so I turned to my wife and I said, 'What can we *do?*' So I moved to New York, and in just one day I increased the population by ten and a half—my opponent has just sixty days to match that record."

Because Bobby Kennedy had been preceded to New York by a reputation of ruthlessness and cynicism, his 1964 Senatorial campaign planners informed him that they would attempt to portray him to the television audience as a sincere, generous man.

Queried Kennedy, "You going to use a double?"

At Riverdale, Long Island on one of Robert Kennedy's 1964 campaign stops, a young lad shouted to the candidate, "Go back where you came from!"

Kennedy, by this time an old hand at fielding these carpetbagger accusations, responded, "People have been telling me that all week—and that's why I'm here."

In a campaign visit to the famed Grossinger's resort hotel in New York State, Robert F. Kennedy addressed a gathering of guests thusly:

"The Catskills were immortalized by Washington Irving. He wrote of a man who fell asleep and awoke in another era. The only other area that can boast such a man is Phoenix, Arizona. . . . Barry Goldwater wants to give control of nuclear weapons to commanders in the field. Now that's my idea of high adventure. General Eisenhower says that he could *live* with a Goldwater Administration. Well, I suppose he'd have as good a chance as anyone else."

About to depart on one of his upstate swings in the 1964 Senatorial race, Robert Kennedy asked one reporter if he would be able to join the entourage. The reporter replied that he would be unable to come because he had previous commitments in Boston.

"Never heard of it," cracked Bobby.

Near the end of his 1964 Senatorial campaign in New York, Robert Kennedy sent a sample of his handwriting—barely legible at best—to a handwriting analyst. The sample said, "If you tell your readers what you see in my handwriting, you'll cost me the election."

During his campaign rally in Riverdale, Long Island candidate Robert Kennedy paused to count the number of Goldwater signs in the crowd. "One, two, three, four, five, six—I've been all up and down the state and that's the most Goldwater people I've seen in one place. I think they were flown in from Albany."